거의 모든 행동 표현의 영어

圖解英語會話
關鍵動詞

謝宜倫——譯

徐寧助——著

音檔
使用說明

STEP ①

[QR Code]

掃描上方 QRCode

STEP ②

立即註冊

👤 帳號　限3-21碼小寫英文數字

✉ 信箱

🔒 密碼　8-24碼小寫英文數字

　　　再次輸入密碼

完成

─────────
社群帳號註冊

f 使用Facebook註冊

G oogle 使用Gooje註冊

快速註冊或登入 EZCourse

[EZCourse 聆聽最新英日韓]

👤 帳號　請輸入電子郵件

🔒 密碼　請輸入密碼

登入

快速註冊 | 忘記密碼

或

f 使用Facebook登入

G oogle 使用Gooie登入

STEP ③

請回答以下問題完成訂閱

一、請問本書第65頁，紅色框線中的英文＿＿是什麼？

二、請問本書第33頁，紅色框線中的英文＿＿是什麼？

答案　請注意大小寫

送出

回答問題按送出

答案就在書中（需注意空格與大小寫）。

STEP ④

完成訂閱

該書右側會顯示「**已訂閱**」，表示已成功訂閱，即可點選播放本書音檔。

STEP ⑤

帳號設定

‹ 個人檔案 ›

EZCourse

點選個人檔案

查看「**我的訂閱紀錄**」會顯示已訂閱本書，點選封面可到本書線上聆聽。

這個動作的英文怎麼說？

第一次學英文的孩子會有很多的疑問，他們想知道眼睛所看見的一切該如何用英文表達。在學習了物品的英文名稱後，更加好奇如何用英文描述動作。例如，他們想知道「挖鼻孔」、「伸長手臂」等動作的英文該怎麼說。那麼學習英文超過十年的成人呢？如果問他們如何用英文說「挖鼻孔」、「伸長手臂」，是無法馬上回答出來的。雖然知道很多難度高的英文單字，卻常發生無法用英文描述日常動作的情況，即便這些動作表達都不難。

本書就是一本告訴我們如何用英文表達這些日常動作的書。可能有人認為「有必要另外花時間學習表達動作的英文嗎？」答案是「有必要！」動作在英語會話中佔了很大的比例。想想看韓國人彼此對話時會說哪些內容呢？早上上班時說著昨晚睡不著、輾轉難眠，或是說錯過了地鐵等等。被問到週末做了些什麼時，對話中可能提到在 Netflix 上看電影，或是去露營。接到朋友來電時，會告訴對方自己正在晾衣服，或說正在邊看電視邊吃晚餐。這一切都是描述動作的詞彙。

當對話的同事或朋友是外國人時，也是大同小異，不同的只是把說話的內容從韓語轉變成英語。因此，想學好英語會話，就必須能夠自由地用英文表達我們做的動作。本書就是將這些英文動作詞彙集結成冊，提供讀者一條捷徑。

人們在學習時，若以自己熟悉的領域作為基礎，將能輕鬆地接受新的內容並進入下一個學習階段。在學習英文單字時，我們從自己周邊的日常單字逐漸擴大範圍到高級詞彙。英語會話也是從自己精通、熟悉的話題開始，逐漸進展到抽象的內容。最理想的是把一輩子可能一次都用不到的內容延後學習，先從切身相關的日常「動作」開始，練習用英文表達出來。

大部分的人都想學好英文。所謂英文好的基準可能有好幾種，但最基本的是能夠流暢無阻地說出想說的話，這也是我們需要知道各種英文動作詞彙的原因。如果能夠明確表達出我過去做過的、我在做的、我將要做的「動作」，便已具備邁向更高級會話境界的基礎。

基於這些原因，《圖解英語會話關鍵動詞》將英語會話的基本表達大致分為「身體部位動作表達」、「日常生活動作表達」、「社會生活動作表達」，同時附上動作圖示。熟悉的詞彙和對應的圖示有助於讀者在沒有學習負擔的情境下，輕鬆接受並記憶書中內容。當讀者沉浸在翻閱圖示的樂趣時，將忍不住驚嘆說：「啊，原來這個動作的英文是這樣說的啊！」、「連這個動作都有英文詞彙呢！」

如果讀者到目前為止不曾從頭到尾讀完一本英文讀物，那麼就以讀完本書作為目標吧！請拋開想把每一個詞彙都背起來的壓力或貪念。請翻一翻各頁，找到感興趣的地方再學習。如果有特別想知道如何表達的詞彙，可以試著搜尋索引。用這樣的方式學習，有一天你將發現，有許多英文動作的詞彙都已不知不覺成為自己的一部分。

筆者在此為各位的英文學習加油！

本書架構與使用方法

本書分成3部分，共17章。PART 1是與我們身體各部位相關的動作表達，PART 2是日常生活中的動作表達，PART 3是社會、職場生活中的動作表達。

本書並非一定要從頭讀到尾。當然，如果喜歡從頭循序漸進地學習也是不錯的方法，但不這麼做也無妨。讀者可以翻閱目錄，找到有興趣的部分或感到好奇的部份先學習。

羅馬不是一天造成的，學習英文也是如此。本書不能只讀一遍，必須反覆多次閱讀。對於已經知道的用法，只要確認過可以跳到下一個，但是若是不知道的用法，就要反覆翻閱多次，才能真正成為自己的知識。此時不能只在腦中讀過，必須開口大聲唸出來，學習效果更佳。

我推薦的學習方法是先讀各個動作的意思，想一想怎麼用英文表達後，再確認書中的英文詞彙。如果學習已經到達一定程度時，可以翻到索引並遮住英文，試著自己用英文表達；或是遮住中文，自己去翻譯英文的意思。這樣的過程有助於讓這些動作的英文詞彙完全屬於自己。

書中標記說明

1. [ ] 表示可以替換前面的單字。

　　例 raise[lift] one's head，可以説 raise one's head 或 lift one's head。

2. ( ) 表示可以一起讀其中的單字或是搭配用法。

　　例 knit one's (eye)brows 可以説 knit one's eyebrows 或 knit one's brows；wink (at ~) 的 at 則是搭配介系詞。

3. / 表示替換單字後，句意可能改變。

　　例 bend over the desk/table 是 bend over the desk 和 bend over the table。

以下是提升英語會話實力必備的《圖解英語會話關鍵動詞》內容架構。

提供英文母語人士以正確的發音所錄製的詞彙和 SENTENCES TO USE 的英文句子。

本文標示順序為中文—英文。以 take a hot/cold shower 為例，出現這樣的標示時，表示 take a hot shower, take a cold shower，意即替換成其他單字後，句意便改變。

soak in a[the] bath 表示 soak in a bath, soak in the bath，意即句意不會隨著替換不同的單字而改變。這種情況下，錄音只錄製了 soak in a bath。

SENTENCES TO USE 是把上方學到的動詞片語實際應用於會話句中的範例。

如果學習已經到達一定程度時，可以訓練自己利用索引複習。將索引中的中文意思遮住來猜測中文；或是將英文片語遮住來猜測英文。此過程有助於使各位的詞彙實力成長到令人刮目相看的地步。

PART 1 身體部位動作表達

CHAPTER 1 臉部 FACE

CHAPTER 2 上半身 UPPER BODY

CHAPTER 3 下半身 LOWER BODY

CHAPTER 4 全身 WHOLE BODY

PART 2　日常生活動作表達

CHAPTER 1　衣著 CLOTHING

CHAPTER 2　飲食 FOOD

CHAPTER 3　外食 EATING OUT

CHAPTER 4　住家 HOUSE

CHAPTER 5　健康與疾病 HEALTH & DISEASE

PART 3 社會生活動作表達

CHAPTER 1　情感表達與人際關係 EMOTIONS & RELATIONSHIP

CHAPTER 2　工作與職業 WORKS & JOBS

CHAPTER 3　購物 SHOPPING

CHAPTER 4　生產與育兒 CHILDBIRTH & PARENTING

CHAPTER 5　休閒與興趣 LEISURE & HOBBIES

PART I

身體部位

動作表達

CHAPTER

1

臉部
FACE

頭（head）

抬頭
raise[lift] one's head

低頭
lower one's head

點頭
nod one's head
搖頭
shake one's head

轉頭（轉向～）
turn one's
head (toward(s) ~)

把頭向後仰
tilt one's head
back(wards)

頭（向後、向前、向左／右）微微傾斜
tilt one's head (back(wards), forward,
to the left/right)

連連點頭
bob
one's head

歪著頭
cock
one's head

伸出頭
stick
one's head out

SENTENCES TO USE

抬起頭，深呼吸。
聽著他的說明，她緩慢地點著頭。
我們把頭轉向發出聲音的地方。
她把頭向後仰，感受雨水打在她的臉上。
孩子把頭伸出門外。

Raise your head and take a deep breath.
Listening to his explanation, she nodded her head slowly.
We turned our heads towards the sound.
She tilted her head back and felt the rain on her face.
The child stuck his head out the door.

2 頭(**head**, **brain**)

*scratch one's head 也表示「聚精會神地思考、尋找難題的解答」。

低下頭、彎腰低頭打招呼
bow
one's head

（因傷腦筋而）抓頭
scratch
one's head

輕拍～的頭、輕撫～的頭髮
pat someone on the head,
stroke one's hair

擊打～的頭部
hit someone
on the head

頭部受傷
hurt one's head,
get hurt on the head,
have a head injury

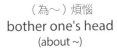

*通常會使用 don't bother your head about ~此句型。

（為～）煩惱
bother one's head
(about ~)

動腦筋、好好想想
use one's brain,
put one's brain to work

絞盡腦汁
rack one's
brain(s)

SENTENCES TO USE

那位政治人物向聚集的市民低頭。　The politician bowed his head to the crowd of citizens.

他抓著頭，不知道說什麼才好。　He scratched his head, unable to find anything to say.

她輕拍著孩子的頭。　She patted the child on the head.

他在車禍中傷到頭部。　He hurt his head in the car accident.

別這樣，動動腦筋。　Come on, use your brain.

3 頭髮（hair）

洗頭
wash[shampoo]
one's hair,
have a shampoo

沖洗頭髮
rinse one's hair

用毛巾把頭髮
包起來
wrap one's hair
in a towel

吹乾頭髮
dry one's hair

梳頭髮
comb[brush]
one's hair

剪頭髮
have[get] one's hair
cut, have[get]
a haircut

剃光頭
have[get] one's hair
shaved off, have[get]
one's head shaved

修剪頭髮
have[get]
one's hair
trimmed

燙頭髮
have[get] one's
hair permed,
have a perm

染頭髮

做頭髮

（自己）
dye one's
hair

（委託他人）
get[have] one's
hair dyed

（自己）
do one's
hair

（在美髮店）
get[have] one's
hair done

拔白髮
pull out [pluck, tweeze,
remove] a gray hair

SENTENCES TO USE

在睡前擦乾你的頭髮。
他去了新開的美髮店剪頭髮。
我媽媽一個月染髮一次。
我現在在做頭髮，因為晚上有約會。

Dry your hair well before you go to bed.
He had his hair cut at the new hair salon.
My mom dyes her hair once a month.
I'm doing my hair since I have a date this
evening.

把頭髮留長
grow out one's hair, let one's hair grow

把頭髮往後綁
tie[put] one's hair back

綁馬尾（動作）
tie[put] one's hair in(to) a ponytail

綁著馬尾（狀態）
wear a ponytail, have[wear] one's hair in a ponytail

綁辮子
braid one's hair

把頭髮盤成高髻
do one's hair up, make a bun

把頭髮放下來
let one's hair down

把頭髮（往左／右）旁分
part one's hair (to[on] the left/right)

把頭髮弄亂
mess up one's hair

（因感到絕望或痛苦而）扯頭髮
tear one's hair out

掉頭髮
lose (one's) hair, hair falls out

植髮
get a hair transplant

SENTENCES TO USE

我在考慮把頭髮留長。	I'm thinking about growing out my hair.
女孩用橡皮筋把頭髮綁在後面。	The girl tied her hair back with a rubber band.
那女子綁著馬尾。	The woman was wearing a ponytail.
他通常將頭髮向左旁分。	He usually parts his hair to the left.
他不知所措地扯著他的頭髮。	Not knowing what to do, he tore his hair out.
我最近頭髮掉得太多了。	I've been losing too much hair lately.

額頭

額頭緊皺
wrinkle one's forehead

擦拭額頭上的汗水
wipe the sweat off one's forehead

輕敲額頭
tap one's forehead

摸額頭（看是否發燒）
feel one's[someone's] forehead
(to see if one[someone] has a fever)

拍額頭
slap one's forehead

頭靠在一起（商量）
put our/your/their heads together

眉毛

（用鑷子）拔眉毛
pluck[pull out]
one's eyebrows
(with tweezers)

皺眉頭
frown,
knit one's
(eye)brows

揚起眉毛（表示慌張、
驚訝、輕蔑）
raise one's
eyebrows

畫眉毛
draw on
one's eyebrows

剃眉毛
shave (off)
one's
eyebrows

SENTENCES TO USE

不要皺著額頭，會生皺紋。
他用手背擦拭額頭的汗水。
她摸摸孩子的額頭，看看他是否發燒。
我忍不住對他們的行為皺眉頭。
她每天早上都畫眉毛。

Don't wrinkle your forehead. You'll get permanent wrinkles.
He wiped the sweat off his forehead with the back of his hand.
She felt her child's forehead to see if he had a fever.
I couldn't help but frown at their behavior.
She draws on her eyebrows every morning.

眼睛

閉上眼睛
close[shut]
one's eyes

輕輕地 / 悄悄地閉起眼睛
close one's eyes
softly/gently

張開眼睛
open one's eyes

翻白眼（表示無聊、
煩躁、不滿）
roll one's eyes

斜著眼睛看、用懷疑的
眼光看
look askance at ~

怒視、瞪視
look angrily[sharply] at ~,
glare at ~

轉移視線
avert[turn away]
one's eyes, look away

用眼角餘光看、瞥見
look out of the corner
of one's eyes

SENTENCES TO USE

看到恐怖的場面時，我閉上眼睛。

聽到他吹噓自己，她翻了一個白眼。

如今許多人對在公家機關工作
的人投以懷疑的眼光。

她沒有回答我的問題，只是瞪著我看。

他發現我在看他，我趕緊轉移目光。

I closed my eyes during the scary scene.

Hearing him brag about himself, she rolled her eyes.

These days, many people look askance at the
people working in the public sector.

She didn't answer my question and just glared at me.

He caught me looking at him, so I quickly averted my eyes.

眨眼
blink (one's eyes)

瞇起眼睛、瞇著眼
squint (at ~), narrow one's eyes

眨一隻眼、（對～）眨眼示意
wink (at ~)

眼睛不眨一下
not bat an eye

垂下眼睛、往下看
lower one's eyes,
look down

揉眼睛
rub one's eyes

遮住眼睛
cover one's eyes

睡覺、小睡片刻
sleep, have a sleep,
take[have] a nap

SENTENCES TO USE

她瞇著眼看招牌。   She squinted at the sign.

詹姆士經過我時對我眨眼示意。   James winked at me as he passed by.

他說話時常常眨眼睛。   He often blinked as he talked.

小孩垂下眼，一語不發。   The child lowered his eyes and said nothing.

不要太常揉眼睛。   Don't rub your eyes too often.

打呼
snore

擦鼻子（鼻涕）
wipe one's (runny) nose

挖（摳）鼻孔
pick one's nose

擤鼻涕
blow
one's nose

吸鼻涕、抽噎
sniffle

（憤怒地）張大鼻孔
flare
one's nostrils

抓鼻子
scratch one's
nose

埋頭、專心於～
have one's nose in ~
（表示專注地閱讀書籍、雜誌或報紙）

付出很高的代價
pay dearly
（舊式用法）

SENTENCES TO USE

她無法和丈夫一起睡，
因為他打呼聲太大。

She can't sleep with her husband because he snores
so loudly.

那孩子看漫畫的時候一直挖鼻孔。

The child keeps picking his nose while reading comic books.

不要再吸鼻子了，去擤鼻涕。

Stop sniffling and blow your nose.

如果一個人抓他或她的鼻子，
代表他或她在說謊。

If a person scratches his or her nose, it means he or
she is lying.

每到週末，那女孩總是在埋頭讀書。

On weekends, the girl always has her nose in the book.

6 嘴巴（**mouth**），嘴唇（**lip**）

 006

嘴巴

閉嘴巴
shut one's mouth,
close one's mouth

閉緊嘴巴
shut one's
mouth firmly[tight]

用手捂住嘴巴
put one's hand over one's mouth,
cover one's mouth with one's hand

張口、開口說話、
鬆口提起
open one's
mouth

張大嘴巴
open one's
mouth wide

擦嘴巴
wipe one's
mouth

親吻
kiss

統一說詞（口徑）
get one's story
straight

咕噥
mumble

SENTENCES TO USE

閉上嘴，吃你的飯。 Shut your mouth and eat your meal.

他緊閉著嘴，什麼話也沒說。 He shut his mouth firmly and said nothing.

請閉上你的眼睛，張開口。 Please close your eyes and open your mouth.

她用紙巾擦她的嘴。 She wiped her mouth with a tissue.

她輕輕地親吻他的臉頰。 She kissed him lightly on his cheek.

嘴唇

舔嘴唇、垂涎某事物
lick one's lips

咬嘴唇
bite one's lip

噘嘴
purse one's lips

噘嘴、嘴嘟得高高的
pout

嘴唇發抖
one's lips quiver

將手指放在嘴唇上
put[lay] one's finger to one's lips
（示意不要說話）

塗抹～在嘴唇上
apply ~ to one's lips,
put ~ on one's lips

SENTENCES TO USE

想到美味的食物，他舔了舔嘴唇。

Thinking of delicious foods, he licked his lips.

她有咬嘴唇的習慣。

She has a habit of biting her lip.

當媽媽不准那孩子玩遊戲時，
他把嘴噘得高高的。

The child pouted when his mother
prevented him from playing the game.

那女子把手指放在嘴唇上說：「噓！」

The woman put her finger to her lips and said, "Shh!"

你的嘴唇很乾。在嘴唇上塗些唇蜜。

Your lips are dry. Apply some lip gloss to your lips.

 舌頭

咬舌頭、忍住想說的話
bite one's tongue

（對～）吐舌頭
stick one's tongue out (at ~)

伸縮舌頭
stick one's tongue out a lot,
dart one's tongue
in and out

咂嘴發出嘖嘖聲
click one's tongue

捲起舌頭
roll one's tongue

嚼舌根、喋喋不休、
胡說八道
wag one's tongue

（小狗等）伸舌頭
have[stick] one's
tongue out

伸舌頭
with one's
tongue out

SENTENCES TO USE

我吃得太快，咬到了舌頭。

那孩子向他媽媽吐了舌頭後跑走了。

我媽媽聽了我的話之後發出嘖嘖聲。

他不停地嚼舌根。

由於天氣太熱，
那隻狗伸著舌頭趴在地上。

I bit my tongue while eating too quickly.

The child stuck his tongue out at his mother and ran away.

My mom clicked her tongue when she heard me.

He kept wagging his tongue.

Because of the hot weather, the dog was lying on
its stomach with its tongue out.

刷牙
brush one's teeth

使用牙線
floss (one's teeth),
use dental floss

使用牙間刷
use an interdental
(tooth)brush

拔牙
have a tooth
removed[pulled (out)]

治療牙齒
have one's
tooth[teeth]
treated

鑲上金牙冠
have[get] one's tooth[teeth]
crowned with gold

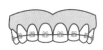

矯正牙齒、戴牙套
have[get] one's
teeth straightened,
wear[have] braces

洗牙
have one's
teeth scaled

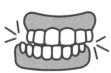

磨牙
grind
one's teeth

咬牙切齒
gnash one's
teeth

咬緊牙關
clench one's
jaw

（用牙籤）剔牙
pick one's teeth

SENTENCES TO USE

你應該在刷牙後使用牙線或牙間刷。 You should floss or use an interdental brush after brushing your teeth.

我昨天拔了一顆智齒。 I had one of my wisdom teeth removed yesterday.

那孩子戴著牙套。 The child is wearing braces.

你最好每年都洗牙。 You should have your teeth scaled every year.

他睡覺的時候會磨牙。 He grinds his teeth when he sleeps.

痛得我必須咬緊牙關。 The pain was so bad that I had to clench my jaw.

耳朵（**ear**），下巴（**chin**），臉頰（**cheek**）

 008

耳朵

仔細聽
listen carefully
to ~

掩耳不聞
close one's ears
to ~

（挖）掏耳朵
pick one's
ear(s)

穿耳洞
have[get]
one's ear(s)
pierced

拉扯耳朵
pull
someone's ear

下巴

抬起下巴
lift[raise] one's chin,
hold one's chin up high

伸出下巴
stick out one's chin

收低下巴
pull one's chin
down

觸碰下巴　　搓揉下巴
touch one's chin　rub one's chin

用手托住下巴
hold one's chin in one's hand(s),
cup one's chin in one's hands

* **chin** 和 **jaw**

chin 和 jaw 都稱為「下巴」，不過兩者的差別在於 jaw 指的是耳下的下半臉，指整個上顎、下顎部位，而 chin 是指 jaw 的下端部位。

SENTENCES TO USE

他對老闆的抱怨充耳不聞。
He closed his ears to his boss's complaints.

他總是在人前用手指掏耳朵。
He keeps picking his ears with his fingers in front of people.

我在20歲時穿耳洞。
I had my ears pierced when I was 20 years old.

這位男性候選人總是在辯論會發言時抬起下巴。
The male candidate raised his chin whenever he spoke at the debate.

她用手托著她的下巴。
She was holding her chin in her hand.

臉紅
turn red, blush

（互相）磨蹭臉頰
rub one's cheek (against someone's)

輕撫臉頰
stroke one's[someone's] cheek

鼓起臉頰
puff out one's
cheeks

用舌頭鼓起一側臉頰
put[stick] one's tongue
in one's cheek

打耳光
slap someone on the cheek[face],
slap someone's cheek[face]

捏臉頰
pinch someone's cheek,
give someone a pinch on the cheek

SENTENCES TO USE

那女孩聽到稱讚後臉紅了。 The girl blushed when she heard the compliment.

那女子用臉頰磨蹭嬰兒的臉頰。 The woman rubbed her cheek against the baby's.

我輕撫著貓咪的臉頰。 I stroked the cat's cheek.

那孩子鼓著臉頰，好像很無聊。 The child was puffing out his cheeks as if bored.

那男子捏著男孩的臉頰，並說他很可愛。 The man pinched the boy's cheek, saying he was cute.

頸部(**neck**), 喉嚨(**throat**)

009

轉動脖子
screw one's head around

按摩脖子
massage someone's
[one's] neck

脖子後仰
bend[lean] one's
neck back(ward)

開嗓子
warm up one's voice

清嗓子
clear one's throat

喉嚨因〜噎住
choke on ~

掐住〜的喉嚨　　掐住〜的喉部使窒息而死
choke someone　　strangle someone,
　　　　　　　choke someone to death

上吊
hang oneself

SENTENCES TO USE

我因為脖子疼痛而按摩後頸。

那位歌手在唱歌前清了清嗓子。

為了休息一下，我坐在椅子上並把脖子往後仰。

那犯人勒死了被害人。

那人上吊自殺但沒有死。

I massaged the back of my neck because it hurt.

The singer cleared her throat before singing.

To rest for a while, I sat in a chair and leaned my neck back.

The criminal strangled the victim.

The man hanged himself but he didn't die.

10 臉部表情(facial expression)

 010

皺著臉
make a face,
frown

微笑
smile

露齒而笑
grin

笑出聲
laugh

咯咯地笑、吃吃地笑
giggle

嘲笑、譏笑
laugh at, mock, ridicule,
sneer at, make fun of

眨一隻眼
wink

皺鼻子
wrinkle one's nose

哭泣
weep, cry

啜泣
sob, cry

臉紅
blush, turn red

翻白眼
（表示無聊、煩躁、不滿）
roll one's eyes

SENTENCES TO USE

孩子對著藥愁眉苦臉。　　　The child frowned at the medicine.

那男子對他的小孩咧嘴一笑。　The man grinned at his little boy.

他一邊讀書一邊咯咯地笑。　　He giggled as he read a book.

她聞到廚餘味道時皺起了鼻子。　She wrinkled her nose when she smelled the food waste.

許多人看到電影中的那一幕都哭了。　Many people sobbed at that scene in the movie.

CHAPTER

2

上半身

UPPER BODY

肩膀（**shoulder**）

聲肩
shrug
(one's shoulders)

聳動肩膀
move one's shoulders
up and down

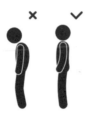

挺直肩膀
straighten one's
shoulders

縮著肩膀
hunch one's
shoulders

按摩肩膀
massage someone's
shoulders

拍拍～的肩膀
pat someone
on the shoulder

摟肩
embrace someone's
shoulder

背（扛）～在肩上
carry ~ on[over]
one's shoulder

勾肩搭背
put arms around
each other's
shoulders

勾肩搭背
with one's arms
around each other's
shoulders

肩並肩站立
stand shoulder to
shoulder

並駕齊驅
rank with,
be equal to

SENTENCES TO USE

茱莉亞對於他的問題默默地聳聳肩。　　Julia shrugged silently at his question.

由於天氣寒冷，她縮著肩膀走路。　　She walked hunching her shoulders as it was cold.

那女孩常常按摩她祖母的肩膀。　　The girl often massages her grandmother's shoulders.

老師拍拍那學生的肩膀。　　The teacher patted the student on the shoulder.

那兩個孩子勾肩搭背地走著。　　The two children walked with their arms around each other's shoulders.

2 手臂(**arms**), 手肘(**elbow**)

手臂

高舉（兩）手臂
raise one's arm(s)

放下（兩）手臂
lower one's arm(s)

打開雙臂
open one's arms

敞開雙臂
with one's arms open

伸出手臂
reach[stretch] out one's arm(s)

雙臂向前伸直
extend one's arms

彎曲手臂
bend one's arm(s)

彎曲手臂並繃緊肌肉
flex one's arm

揮動雙臂
swing one's arms

挽起袖子
roll[turn] up one's sleeves

枕臂側躺
lie with one's arm under one's head,
lie using one's arm as a pillow

SENTENCES TO USE

將雙臂伸直舉高過頭部。

那孩子張開雙臂跑過來。

我伸出雙臂，將箱子從壁櫃上拿下來。

他彎曲手臂並繃緊，以展示他的肌肉。

他挽起袖子並開始搬運箱子。

Raise your arms straight above your head.

The child came running with his arms open wide.

I stretched out my arms and lowered the box from the closet shelf.

He flexed his arm to show off his muscles.

He rolled up his sleeves and started carrying the boxes.

抓住～的手臂
hold[grab] someone's arm,
hold[take, catch, seize]
someone by the arm

甩開～的手臂
shake off someone's arm

拉著～的手臂
pull someone's arm

緊緊抓住～的手臂
cling to someone's arm

（獨自）雙臂抱胸
fold one's arms

（獨自）雙臂抱胸
with one's arms folded

（與他人）勾手臂
lock one's arms
together

（與他人）手臂挽著手臂
arm in arm (with ~)

扭～的手臂
twist someone's arm

SENTENCES TO USE

有人抓住我的手臂叫我的名字。
她雙臂抱胸陷入沉思。
他和他的媽媽手臂挽著手臂走著。

Someone grabbed my arm and called my name.
She was lost in thought with her arms folded.
He was walking arm in arm with his mother.

手肘放在～上
put elbows on ~

手肘放在～上
with elbows on ~

用手肘輕推、擠
nudge[jog, jostle] with
one's elbow

以手肘擠著向前走
elbow one's way through ~

SENTENCES TO USE

吃飯時，手肘放在桌上被認為是不禮貌的。

他用手肘擠過人群。

It is considered rude to eat with your elbows on the table.

He elbowed his way through the crowd.

手腕

抓住～的手腕
hold[grab] someone's wrist,
hold[take, grab, catch, seize]
someone by the wrist

扭轉手腕
turn
one's wrist

扭傷手腕
sprain
one's wrist

手

舉手
raise
one's hand

舉手
with
one's hand(s) up

手放下
lower
one's hand

與～握手
shake hands (with ~)

牽～的手
hold someone's
hand

（兩人）牽手
hold each
other's hands

牽手
hand in hand

雙手十指交叉
clasp one's hands

SENTENCES TO USE

當他抓住我的手腕時，我的心臟怦怦直跳。　My heart was pounding when he grabbed my wrist.
他在打籃球時扭傷手腕。　He sprained his wrist playing basketball.
那孩子舉著手過行人穿越道。　The child crossed the crosswalk with his hand up.
市長和與會者握手。　The mayor shook hands with the attendees.
那孩子牽著她媽媽的手。　The child is holding her mother's hand.

握緊拳頭
clench
one's fist(s)

合掌於胸前
put[have] one's hands
together in front of the
chest[as if in prayer]

張開手
open
one's hand

用手遮擋陽光
shade the sun with
one's hand(s)

把手放入～
put one's hand in ~

把手從～拿出
take one's hand
out of ~

洗手
wash one's
hands

揮手
wave one's
hand

緊抓～的手
grasp someone's hand

甩開～的手
shake off
someone's hand

向～伸出手
reach[stretch, hold]
out one's hand to ~

SENTENCES TO USE

當他聽到這個故事時，氣得握緊拳頭。 He clenched his fist in anger when he heard the story.

他把手從口袋裡拿出來。 He took his hand out of his pocket.

人們向沿著跑道降落滑行的飛機揮手。 The people waved their hands at the plane going down the runway.

她甩開他的手並尖叫起來。 She shook off his hand and screamed.

走在前面的人向我伸出手。 The person who was going up ahead reached out his hand to me.

雙手叉腰
put one's hands
on one's hips

雙手叉腰
with one's hands
on one's hips

手顫抖
hands
tremble[shake]

搓手
rub one's
hands (together)

呼呼地吹著手
blow on
one's hands

手背、手掌

用火烘手取暖
warm one's hands
by[over] the fire

用手背擦拭額頭上的汗水
wipe the sweat off one's forehead
with the back of one's hand

用手背擦嘴
wipe one's mouth with
the back of one's hand

親吻手背
kiss someone's hand,
kiss someone on the
back of someone's hand

擊掌
highfive

（彼此）手掌貼在一起
put our/your/their
palms together

打～的手掌心
hit someone
on the palm

SENTENCES TO USE

超人雙手叉腰站著。 Superman is standing with his hands on his hips.

她緊張到手都在發抖。 She was so nervous that her hands were trembling.

由於手很冰冷，我把兩手搓了搓。 I rubbed my hands together since they were cold.

他用手背擦拭額頭上的汗水。 He wiped the sweat off his forehead with the back of his hand.

在西方，男子親吻女子的手背並不罕見。 In the West, it was not uncommon for men to kiss women on the back of their hands.

4 手指(**finger**), 手指甲(**fingernail**)

 014

手指

張開手指
spread one's
fingers

折手指
fold one's fingers

用手指指著～、對～指指點點
point ~, point one's finger at ~

用手指觸摸
feel ~ with one's
fingers

用手指數算
count ~ on[with]
one's fingers

豎起大拇指
give
a thumbs-up

在手指上戴戒指
put a ring on one's finger（動作）
wear[have] a ring on
one's finger（狀態）

摘下戒指
take one's ring off

SENTENCES TO USE

張開你的手指。你的無名指比食指長。

Spread your fingers. Your ring finger is longer than your index finger.

當我用手指指著月亮時，不要只看著我的手指。

When I point my finger at the moon, don't look only at my finger.

用手指指著別人是不禮貌的。

It's not polite to point your finger at people.

教練對球員豎起大拇指。

The coach gave a thumbs-up to the player.

折手指關節，使發出聲響
crack one's fingers[knuckles]

吸吮手指
suck one's finger, live from hand to mouth
（收入勉強度日）

割破手指
cut one's finger

不做任何事
not lift a finger, not do anything

手指甲

剪指甲
cut[clip] one's (finger)nails (short)

修指甲
trim one's (finger)nails

（因緊張而）咬指甲
bite one's (finger)nails

用指甲抓、劃破
scratch with one's (finger)nails

做指甲
get one's nails done, get a manicure
塗指甲油
manicure one's nails, apply nail polish

指甲斷裂
break one's (finger)nail

指甲脫落
lose one's (finger)nail, one's (finger)nail falls off[falls out]

SENTENCES TO USE

折手指發出聲音對手指不好嗎？	Is cracking your knuckles bad for them?
我的手指被紙劃傷。	I cut my finger on a piece of paper.
指甲不要剪太短。	Don't cut your nails too short.
他最近改掉咬指甲的習慣。	He recently gave up his old habit of biting his nails.
安妮每週都在美甲店做指甲。	Annie gets her nails done at the nail salon every week.

5 背／腰(**back**), 腰部(**waist**), 肚子(**abdomen**, **belly**)

背／腰

| 挺直背
straighten one's back,
straighten[stretch]
oneself | 身體前彎、彎腰
bend forward,
bend down | 鞠躬哈腰、阿諛奉承
kiss someone's
ass | 背向後靠在～
lean back
against ~ |

上半身向後仰
lean back

對～不理睬
turn one's back on[to] ~

拍打～的背
slap a person
on the back

輕拍～的背
pat someone
on the back

用力推～的背
push someone's
back

背上背著～
carry ~ on one's
back

SENTENCES TO USE

把背挺直，看著前方。
Straighten your back and look forward.

你應該學習在不壓迫脊椎的情況下彎腰。
You should learn to bend forward without putting pressure on your spine.

她背靠在沙發上看書。
She is reading a book leaning back against the sofa.

那次事件之後，大多數的人都不理睬他了。
Most people turned their backs on him after the incident.

過去的媽媽們經常把孩子背在背上。
In the past, mothers often carried their baby on their back.

背痛
one's back hurts,
have back pain

抓背
scratch one's back

把聽診器放在背上
put a stethoscope
on one's back

腰

腰受傷
hurt one's back[waist]

閃到腰
put one's back out

扭腰
twist one's waist

繫腰帶
wear a[one's] belt

勒緊腰帶、省吃儉用
tighten a[one's] belt,
draw a belt tighter

表示「腰」的單字
- **back**：背部、背下半部的後腰
- **waist**：腰部凹進去的部位

SENTENCES TO USE

我的背因為坐在桌前太久而疼痛。

他用尺抓背。

醫生把聽診器放在病人背上，
聽她的呼吸。

那個男子在穿鞋子的時候閃到腰。

由於收入減少，我們必須省吃儉用。

My back hurts from sitting at the desk for too long.

He scratched his back with a ruler.

The doctor put a stethoscope on the patient's back to
hear her breathing.

The man put his back out when he was putting on his shoes.

We had to tighten our belts because we were making
less money.

肚子

肚子餓
be hungry

吃飽
be full

肚子痛
have a stomachache

GrOOOWl...

肚子咕嚕咕嚕地叫
one's stomach is growling

挺著肚子
stick out one's belly

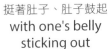

挺著肚子、肚子鼓起
with one's belly sticking out

趴著、俯臥
lie on one's stomach

俯臥
on one's stomach

搓揉肚子
rub one's belly[stomach]

大腹便便
have[get] a potbelly

減掉腹部贅肉
lose belly fat

表示「肚子」的單字
- **stomach**：指稱「肚子」的一般用法，主要用於和「胃」有關的內容。
- **belly**：指稱身體部位的「肚子」。
- **abdomen**：指稱「腹部」的專門用法。

SENTENCES TO USE

我餓得可以吃下一匹馬。
那女子挺著肚子走路。
趴著看書對你的背不好。
小狗喜歡人們搓揉牠們的肚子。
自從我40歲後就有肚子了。

I'm so hungry I could eat a horse.
The woman walks with her belly sticking out.
Reading a book on your stomach is bad for your back.
Puppies like people to rub their belly.
I've had a potbelly since I turned 40.

CHAPTER

3

下半身

LOWER BODY

臀部、屁股(hip, butt), 骨盆(pelvis)

 016

臀部、屁股

擺動屁股
sway one's hips
上下扭動屁股
move one's hips
up and down

搖屁股
shake[rock, swing] one's hips

（從座位上）抬起屁股
lift one's hips

屁股向後移動
move the hips back

拍～的屁股
pat someone
on the hip

抓屁股
scratch one's butt

拍打屁股
slap one's butt, slap
someone on someone's butt

拍打褲子屁股上的灰塵
dust off the
bottom of one's pants

脫下褲子
take down
one's pants

骨盆

扭動骨盆
shake[move]
one's pelvis

把褲子／裙子穿到骨盆處
wear one's pants/
skirt over one's pelvis

hip 和 butt
這兩個字都是「屁股、臀部」，但實際上有
些差異。
• **hip :** 指腰部和腿部之間的骨盆部位
• **butt(buttocks) :** 從背後看上去的圓狀
　凸起部位（屁股）
此外，behind 或 backside、bottom 都
可用來表示「屁股」。

SENTENCES TO USE

那舞者隨著音樂扭動臀部。
那位男演員邊走路邊擺動臀部。
媽媽輕輕拍著嬰兒的屁股。
我的一位朋友打我的屁股。
在跳那支舞時，你必須經常扭動骨盆。

The dancer is shaking his hips to the music.
The actor walks with his hips swaying.
The mother patted the baby on the hip.
A friend of mine slapped me on my butt.
When performing that dance, you have to move your pelvis a lot.

2 腿(leg), 大腿(thigh)

腿

翹腳、翹二郎腿
cross one's legs

sit with one's legs crossed
翹著腿坐

盤腿而坐
sit cross-legged

抖腳
shake one's leg

伸展（伸直）腿
stretch[straighten]
one's legs

把腿伸直
with one's legs
straight

張開雙腿
spread
one's legs

雙腿打開坐著
sit with
one's legs apart

腿併攏
close one's legs

彎著腿
bend one's legs

按摩腿
massage one's legs

抓腿
scratch one's leg

SENTENCES TO USE

翹腳坐對骨盆不好。 Sitting with your legs crossed is bad for your hips.

坐著雙腿伸直，並將你的
上半身往前傾至腿部。 Sit with your legs straight and bend your upper
body over your legs.

有些人在地鐵上張開雙腿坐著。 There are people who sit with their legs apart onthe subway.

把你的腿併攏，給別人騰出一些空間。 Close your legs and make some room.

那女孩按摩她祖母的腿。 The girl massaged her grandmother's legs.

單腳站立
stand on one leg

拖著腿
drag one's leg

跛著（右／左）腿
limp (in the right/left leg),
walk with a limp (on[in] the[one's] right/left leg)

腿麻
have pins and needles in one's leg,
one's leg is numb,
have no feelings in one's leg,
one's leg falls asleep

腿抽筋
have[get] a cramp
in the leg,
get[be] cramped in the leg

腿受傷
hurt[injure]
one's leg

腿斷了
break
one's leg

腿截肢
have one's leg
amputated

腿上打石膏
wear a cast on
one's leg

絆倒～
trip someone (up)

SENTENCES TO USE

你能單腳站立多久？

自從接受背部手術後，
他右腳走路有點跛。

長時間盤腿坐，我的腿都麻了。

他踢足球時腿受了傷。

那男子的腿上打著石膏。

How long can you stand on one leg?

He walks with a slight limp on his right leg
since his back surgery.

After sitting cross-legged for a long time, my legs are numb.

He hurt his leg while playing soccer.

The man is wearing a cast on his leg.

摸～的大腿
stroke someone's thigh

打～的大腿
slap[hit] someone's thigh,
slap[hit] someone on the thigh

捏自己的大腿
pinch one's thigh
捏自己大腿一下，看看是不是在做夢
pinch oneself to see if one is dreaming

SENTENCES TO USE

她大聲地笑並拍打旁邊朋友的大腿。

我必須準備考試，但實在太睏了，
所以我捏自己的大腿。

She laughed out loud and slapped her friend next to her on the thigh.

I had to study for the exam, but I was very sleepy, so I pinched my thigh.

UNIT 3

膝蓋(**knee**, **lap**), 小腿後側(**calf**),
小腿前側(**shin**)

 018

膝蓋

彎曲膝蓋
bend one's
knees

向上屈膝
draw up
one's knees

向上屈膝
with one's
knees up

抱膝
hug one's knees,
put one's arms
around one's knees

單膝跪地
go down on
one knee

下跪
kneel down, go[fall]
down on one's knees,
drop to[on] one's knees

跪下
on one's
knees

和～促膝談心
get knee to
knee with ～

促膝
knee to knee

跪步膝行
go on one's
knees

躺在～的腿上
lie on someone's lap,
lay[rest] one's head on[in]
someone's lap

拍打大腿
slap[hit]
someone's lap

膝蓋破皮
have[get] one's knee(s)
skinned[scraped],
scrape one's knee(s)

knee 和 lap

兩者都有「膝部」的意思，但
並不相同。

· knee：腿部彎折的部位
· lap：坐下來時，腰到膝蓋之
間的大腿部位

SENTENCES TO USE

在做那個姿勢時，
你必須把膝蓋彎曲90度。

You have to bend your knees 90 degrees
when you do that position.

她抱膝坐在地上。

She was sitting on the floor hugging her knees.

他跪下來，撿起在地上的紙。

He knelt down to pick up the paper from the floor.

我還穿著鞋子，所以跪著進入房間。

I entered the room on my knees because I still had my shoes on.

他躺在草地上，頭枕在女朋友的膝上。

He was lying on his girlfriend's lap on the lawn.

按摩小腿肚
massage one's calves

打～的小腿肚
hit[whip, lash] someone's calves

小腿肚被打到
get hit[whipped, lashed] on the calves

小腿前側

踢～的小腿前側
kick someone in the shin

小腿前側撞到～
bump[hit] one's shin against ~

calf 和 shin
- calf（小腿後側）：小腿（膝蓋到腳踝之間）後方部位
- shin（小腿前側）：小腿（膝蓋到腳踝之間）前方帶有
骨頭的部位

小腿前側擦破
have[get] one's shin scraped[skinned]

SENTENCES TO USE

在跑步之後，我按摩我的小腿肚。

我小時候做錯事時，
就會被父母打小腿肚。

他踢了自己下屬的小腿前側。

我的小腿前側撞到床腳。

在踢足球時，他小腿前側擦傷了。

After running, I massaged my calves.

When I was a child, I got whipped on the calves by my parents if I did something wrong.

He kicked his subordinate in the shin.

I bumped my skin against the corner of the bed.

He got his shin scraped while playing soccer.

腳

絆倒、失足
trip, stumble, lose[miss] one's footing

被～絆倒
trip over

拖著腳
drag one's foot[feet]

按摩腳
massage one's foot[feet]

伸展腳
stretch one's foot[feet]

跺腳
stomp one's foot[feet]

邁開腳步
set foot, take a step (forward)

停下腳步
stop

掉頭
turn back, turn away, turn[direct] one's steps (toward ~)

用腳踢
kick ~

踩踏
step on ~

跟上～的步伐
keep pace with ~, fall into step with ~

做足浴
soak one's feet (in warm water)

SENTENCES TO USE

他在樓梯上摔跤，一路跌了下來。
在電影裡，犯人拖著他的腳。
圖書館關門了，我們得掉頭才行。
穿高跟鞋的女子在地鐵上踩到我的腳。

He tripped on the stairs and tumbled all the way down.
In the movie, the criminal dragged his feet.
The library was closed, so we had to turn away.
A woman in high heels stepped on my foot on the subway.

踏出第一步進入～（開始從事某領域的工作）
take the[one's] first step into ~,
start work in ~

從～抽身（斷絕關係）
wash one's hands of ~,
back out of ~,
sever connections[relations] with ~

斷絕往來
stop visiting ~,
keep away from ~

腳踝

交叉雙腳（腳踝）
cross one's ankles

扭傷腳踝
sprain one's ankle

轉動腳踝
turn one's ankle

伸展腳踝
stretch one's ankle

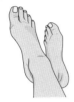

腳踝朝身體方向拉
pull one's ankle
toward one's body

受制於～
be tied to ~,
be chained to ~,
be pressed with ~

（腳踝）戴電子監控腳環
wear an electronic
monitoring anklet

SENTENCES TO USE

作為那樂團的貝斯手，
他邁出踏進音樂界的第一步。

He took his first step into the music scene as
the bassist for that band.

我現在想從整個情況中抽身。

I want to wash my hands of the whole situation.

她交叉著腳踝坐在椅子上。

She was sitting on a chair with her ankles crossed.

我的腳無力，
於是我按摩腳並且轉一轉腳踝。

My feet were tired, so I massaged my feet and
turned my ankles.

伸展你的腳踝，並把它們往自己的身體拉。

Stretch your ankles and pull them toward your body.

腳底

| 搔腳底
tickle the sole of
someone's foot | 抓腳底
scratch the sole
of one's foot | 腳底起水泡
have a blister on the
sole of one's foot | 腳底長繭
have a callus on the
sole of one's foot |

腳跟

提起腳跟
lift one's heel(s)

踮著腳走、用腳尖走
walk on tiptoes

SENTENCES TO USE

我搔他的腳底，但他不為所動。	I tickled the soles of his feet, but he didn't budge.
我穿著新鞋一整天，結果腳底起水泡了。	I've been wearing new shoes all day today, and I've got blisters on the soles of my feet.
那位舞者的腳布滿了繭，包括腳底也是。	The dancer has calluses all over her feet, including the soles.
我們踮著腳尖走路，以免吵醒嬰兒。	We walked on tiptoes in case the baby woke up.

5 腳趾(**toe**), 腳趾甲(**toenail**)

 020

腳趾

扭動腳趾
wiggle[wriggle]
one's toes

張開腳趾
spread[stretch]
one's toes

彎曲腳趾
bend[curl] one's toes

按摩腳趾
massage one's toes

腳趾甲

緊抓腳趾
grasp one's toes

咬腳趾
bite one's toes

剪腳趾甲
clip[cut] one's
toenails

修腳趾甲
trim one's
toenails

塗腳趾甲油
paint one's toenails

腳趾甲脫落
one's toenail falls off,
have one's toenail
fall off

不露聲色，守口如瓶
（比喻）
keep one's cards
close to one's vest

磨利爪子、警戒
周遭（比喻）
sharpen one's
claws

SENTENCES TO USE

小孩一邊看電視一邊擺動腳趾。
The child was watching TV, wiggling his toes.

她張開腳趾塗腳趾甲油。
She was spreading her toes and painting her toenails.

那嬰兒正在咬自己的腳趾。
The baby was biting his toes.

我想我大概每三週剪一次腳趾甲。
I think I cut my toenails about once every three weeks.

之前我因為有一個
腳趾甲脫落而吃盡苦頭。
Once I had a hard time because one of my
toenails fell off.

CHAPTER

4

全身

WHOLE BODY

021

躺下
lie down, lay oneself down

仰面躺下
lie down on one's back, lie face up

側身躺下
lie on one's side, lie down sideways

俯臥
lie on one's stomach, lie face down

蜷縮躺著
lie curled up

輾轉反側
toss and turn

醒來、起床
wake up, get up. get out of bed

從床上跳起來
spring[jump] out of bed

站立、起身
stand up, get up, rise (from ~)

一躍而起
spring[jump] to one's feet, stand up suddenly

筆直站立
stand (up) straight, stand upright

踮著腳站
stand on tiptoes

單腳站立
stand on one leg

用單腳保持平衡
balance oneself on one leg

SENTENCES TO USE

他側躺著睡覺。　　　　　　He was sleeping lying on his side.

那孩子趴在沙發上。　　　　The child was lying face down on the couch.

小狗蜷縮躺著。　　　　　　The puppy is lying curled up.

他輾轉反側，許久後才睡著。　He tossed and turned for a long time before falling asleep.

她一聽到鈴聲馬上一躍而起。　She jumped to her feet when she heard the bell.

你能單腳站立多久？　　　　How long can you stand on one leg?

（向左／右）轉動、
扭動身體
turn[twist] one's body
(to the left／right)

身體前傾
lean forward

身體向左／右傾
lean one's body to
the left/right

身體前彎
bend forward

身體後仰
bend back(wards)

身體向前傾靠著書桌／桌子
bend over the
[one's] desk/table

趴在桌上
sit in the chair and have
one's head on the desk

身體往後靠
lean back

背靠著椅子坐
sit back
in the chair

端正姿勢
straighten (up)
one's posture

搖晃身體
shake[move]
one's body

身體躁動、坐立不安
fidget

SENTENCES TO USE

身體向右轉，並舉起你的左手臂。　　Turn your body to the right and raise your left arm.

她身體向前傾，讀著岩石上的字。　　She leaned forward and read the words on the rock.

他身體向後仰，抬頭望著天空。　　He bent back and looked up at the sky.

他背靠在椅子上小睡片刻。　　He sat back in the chair and took a nap.

一定要一直注意端正你的姿勢。　　Always take care to straighten your posture.

蹲下
crouch down

駝著背、弓著身子
hunch one's body

低下身子
lower one's body,
lower oneself down

蜷縮、縮著身子（捲起背，
四肢緊貼著身體的姿勢）
curl up

身體（因～）顫抖
tremble, shudder,
shake oneself (with ~)

跟跟蹌蹌地走
stagger, stumble

保持身體平衡
keep one's balance

運動
work out, exercise

做暖身運動
warm up,
do warm-up exercises

SENTENCES TO USE

他蹲在郵筒後面躲起來。

在一個寒冷的冬夜，那女子蜷縮在毯子下。

那男子因為喝了很多酒而跟跟蹌蹌地走著。

規律且適當的運動有益健康。

你在跑步以前一定要做熱身運動。

He crouched down behind a post box and hid.

The woman curled up under the blanket on a cold winter's night.

The man staggered because he drank a lot.

It is good for your health to exercise regularly and moderately.

You should warm up before going for a run.

2 身體管理

Shower

保持身體清潔
keep oneself
[one's body] clean

淋浴
shower,
take[have] a shower

沖熱 / 冷水澡
take a hot/cold
shower

在身上塗抹沐浴乳（沐浴露）/ 打肥皂
rub body wash[shower gel]/
soap all over one's body

泡澡
take a bath

泡熱 / 冷水澡
take a hot/
cold bath

身體浸泡在浴池裡
soak in a[the] bath

泡半身浴
take a lower-body bath,
soak one's lower body in warm water

暖身子、取暖
warm oneself up,
get warm

SENTENCES TO USE

總是保持身體清潔是好的。
It's good to keep yourself clean all the time.

即使在夏天，我也無法沖冷水澡。
I can't take a cold shower even in summer.

現在我要回家泡個熱水澡。
Now I'll go home and take a hot bath.

在工作繁忙的日子，
把身體浸泡在熱水裡有助於解除壓力。
On days when I have a lot of work,
soaking in a hot bath helps to relieve stress.

在韓國，很多人泡半身浴。
In Korea, many people take a lower-body bath.

讓身體暖和
keep oneself warm

用毛毯裹住身體
wrap oneself in a blanket

舒服地躺進沙發裡
nestle down into
the sofa[couch]

放鬆身體、消除緊張
relax one's body

失去 / 危害健康
lose/harm[ruin] one's health

恢復健康
get well, get better, recover

保重、照顧自己
take care of oneself

SENTENCES TO USE

請隨時保持身體暖和。
Please try to keep yourself warm all the time.

她正舒服地躺在沙發上看書。
She is reading a book nestling down into the sofa.

如果睡眠不足，可能會危害你的健康。
If you don't get enough sleep, it could harm your health.

他做了腦部手術，現在正在恢復中。
He had brain surgery and is now recovering.

獨自生活的人一定要照顧好自己。
People who live alone should always take care of themselves.

裝飾、打扮自己
adorn oneself

盛裝打扮
get dressed up

照鏡子
look at oneself in the mirror

躲藏、隱身
hide[conceal] oneself

用力推～的身體
push someone's body

搜身
search someone's body

SENTENCES TO USE

他盛裝打扮後去赴約。　He got dressed up and went on a date.

她穿上新衣服並照鏡子。　She put on her new clothes and looked at herself in the mirror.

那個男子讓自己隱身於世。　The man hid himself from the world.

警察對嫌犯搜身。　The police searched the suspect's body.

PART II

1

衣著

CLOTHING

穿衣服

* put on ~ 和
  wear ~ 的後面要接受詞，但
  get dressed 不需要受詞。
  get dressed 本身就是「穿衣服」的
  意思。

穿
put on ~（動作），
get dressed（動作），
wear ~（狀態）

脫
take off ~

把頭伸進～
put one's head in ~

把手臂伸進袖子裡
put one's arm in the sleeve

扣上鈕扣
button (up) ~

解開鈕扣
unbutton ~

拉上褲子拉鍊
zip up one's
fly[pants, trousers]

拉上拉鍊
zip up ~

拉下拉鍊
unzip ~

繫上腰帶
buckle
one's belt

解開腰帶
unbuckle
one's belt

SENTENCES TO USE

他正在穿衣服準備外出。

當她回到家，她就脫下夾克並躺在沙發上。

那孩子正費力地把手臂伸進 T 恤的袖子裡。

我的右手受傷了，因此很難扣上襯衫的扣子。

他上廁所後忘記拉上褲子的拉鍊。

He is getting dressed to go out.

When she got home, she took off her jacket and lay down on the couch.

The child is struggling to put his arm in the sleeve of the T-shirt.

I hurt my right hand, so it's hard to button my shirt.

He forgot to zip up his pants after going to the bathroom.

捲袖子
roll[pull, turn] up
the sleeve

折褲管
roll[pull, turn]
up one's[the]
pants[trousers]

豎起衣領
turn up
the collar

戴帽子

（動作）
put on
a hat[cap]

（狀態）
wear
a hat[cap]

脫帽子
take off one's
hat[cap]

帽子反戴
wear a cap
backwards

戴帽子時把帽子壓低
wear a hat[cap] low
over one's eyes

脖子上圍著圍巾
wear[wrap] a scarf
around one's neck

繫上領帶
tie[wear]
a tie[necktie]

解開領帶
untie[take off]
a tie[necktie]

把領帶拉直
straighten one's
tie[necktie]

戴上袖扣
put on cufflinks

SENTENCES TO USE

天氣很熱，所以他捲起襯衫的袖子。 The weather was hot, so he rolled up the sleeves of his shirt.

那孩子因為褲子太長而把褲管捲起來。 The child rolled up his pants because they were too long.

風很大，於是她把風衣的領子豎起來。 The wind was blowing hard, so she turned up the
collar of her trench coat.

他脫下帽子向老師鞠躬致意。 He took off his hat and bowed to the teacher.

那個犯人把帽子戴得低低的， The criminal was wearing a hat low over his eyes,

以致我們看不清楚他的臉。 so we couldn't make out his face.

戴手套

（動作）
put on (one's)
gloves

（狀態）
wear
gloves

脫下手套
take off (one's)
gloves

穿鞋子

（動作）
put on (one's)
shoes

（狀態）
wear (one's)
shoes

戴耳環 / 項鍊 / 手環 / 戒指

脫鞋子
take off (one's)
shoes

（動作）
put on earrings/
a necklace/a bracelet/a ring

（狀態）
wear earrings/a necklace/
a bracelet/a ring

將～披在肩上
wrap ~ around one's
shoulders

多穿幾件、
使穿得暖和
dress in layers,
bundle up

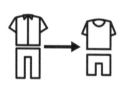
換衣服
change (one's)
clothes

挑選要穿的衣服 / 套裝 / 襯衫
pick out[choose] clothes/
a suit/a shirt ... to wear

SENTENCES TO USE

在韓國，進入屋內時要脫鞋子。

In Korea, you have to take off your shoes when you go inside a house.

她戴上新買的珍珠耳環。

She put on her new pearl earrings.

他把毛衣披在肩上。

He wrapped a sweater around his shoulders.

我今天穿得很暖和，因為天氣很冷。

I bundled up today because it was cold.

他流了很多汗，所以換了衣服。

He had sweat a lot, so he changed his clothes.

2 衣服處理

分類待洗衣物
sort the laundry

把有色衣服和
白色衣服分開
separate the colors
from the whites

洗衣服
wash (one's) clothes,
do the laundry

用洗衣機洗衣服
do the laundry using
the washing machine

用手洗
hand-wash ~,
wash ~ by hand

把待洗衣物放入洗衣機
load the washing machine,
put the laundry in the
washing machine

加入洗衣劑 /
衣物柔軟精
add detergent/
fabric softener

清水洗淨衣服
rinse
the laundry

洗衣脫水
spin-dry the
laundry

從洗衣機取出洗好的衣物
unload the washing machine,
take the laundry out of the
washing machine

抖開（從洗衣機取出的）
衣物
shake out
the laundry

（在曬衣架 / 晾衣繩上）晾衣服
hang (out) the laundry
(on a clothes drying rack/clothesline)

SENTENCES TO USE

我今天必須洗衣服。 I have to do the laundry today.

我手洗我的內衣。 I hand-wash my underwear.

把待洗衣物放進洗衣機之後加入洗衣劑。 Put the laundry in the washing machine and then add detergent.

我要放衣物柔軟精嗎？ Do I have to add fabric softener?

從洗衣機取出洗好的衣服，並且把它們晾乾。 Take the laundry out of the washing machine and hang it out to dry.

收曬好的衣服
get the laundry,
take the laundry off the clothes drying rack[clothesline]

把洗好的衣服放入烘衣機
put the laundry in the dryer

把衣服從烘衣機取出
take the laundry out of the dryer

曬衣服
dry the laundry

摺衣服
fold the laundry

煮待洗衣物
boil clothes
[the laundry]

把～上漿
starch ~

熨燙
iron ~

在～上噴水
spray water on ~

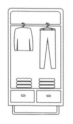

掛～（在衣櫃）
hang up ~

漂白
bleach ~

送～去乾洗
have ~ dry cleaned

SENTENCES TO USE

把衣服從烘衣機取出後，
你必須把它們摺好。

我今天必須熨燙5件襯衫。

在你熨燙衣服以前，
必須先在衣服上噴些水。

請把熨燙好的襯衫掛在衣櫥裡。

白色襯衫需要偶爾進行漂白。

我今天把很多衣服送去乾洗，
包括一件大衣和一件夾克。

After you take the laundry out of the dryer,
you have to fold it.

I need to iron five shirts today.

You have to spray water on your clothes
before ironing them.

Please hang up your ironed shirt in the closet.

White shirts should be bleached occasionally.

I dropped off a bunch of clothes, including a
coat and a jacket, to have them dry cleaned today.

修補衣服
alter[mend]
clothes

修改褲子 / 裙子 / 袖子長度

（自己）
shorten one's pants/
one's skirt/the sleeves

（委託他人）
have one's pants/one's skirt/
the sleeves shortened

修改～的胸圍、腰圍

（自己）
make ~ tighter around
the chest[waist]

（委託他人）
have ~ made tighter
around the chest[waist]

縫紉、縫合
sew, stitch

把線穿過針孔
thread a needle

縫補襪子上的洞
darn one's socks

自己製作衣服
make one's own
clothes, make
clothes oneself

使用縫紉機
use a sewing
machine

在縫紉機上縫～
sew ~ on a sewing
machine

SENTENCES TO USE

我讓裁縫店把裙子改短。 I had my skirt shortened at an alterations shop.

他不會縫衣服。 He doesn't know how to sew.

我補好襪子上的洞後重新穿上。 I darned my socks and wore them again.

那女子有時候自己製作衣服。 The woman sometimes makes her own clothes.

她用縫紉機做了一個墊子。 She made a cushion using a sewing machine.

準備錢幣
have one's
coins ready

把紙鈔換成錢幣
get change

購買洗衣劑和烘衣柔軟去
靜電紙
buy detergent and
fabric softener sheets

選擇洗衣機
choose a
machine

放入待洗衣物
put the laundry
in the washing
machine

加入洗衣劑
add detergent

關上洗衣機門，扭轉手把，
使門密閉
close the door and
turn the handle to seal it

選擇洗衣模式
choose a
laundry cycle

投入錢幣
insert coins

取出洗好的衣物
take the laundry
out of the machine

把洗好的衣物放入烘衣機
put the laundry
in the dryer

加入烘衣柔軟去靜電紙
add fabric softener
sheets

Dry normal,
low heat

Dry normal,
medium heat

Dry normal,
high heat

設定烘衣溫度
set the
drying temperature

按下開始鍵
press the
START button

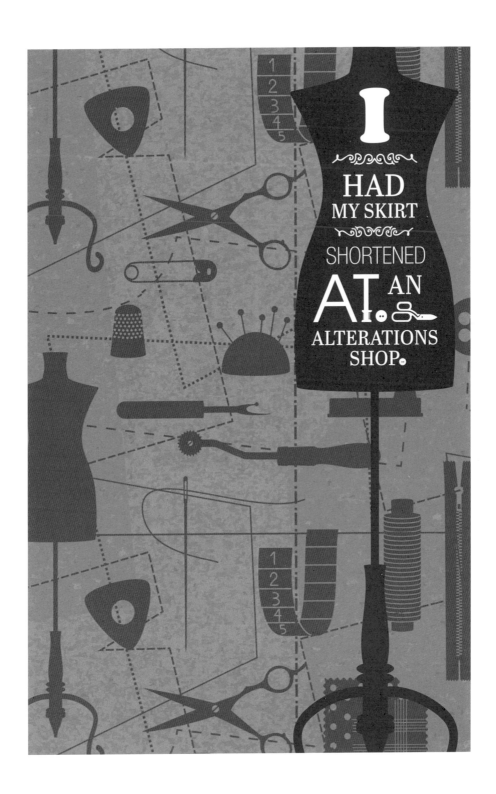

I HAD MY SKIRT SHORTENED AT. AN ALTERATIONS SHOP.

CHAPTER

2

飲食

FOOD

把～放入櫥櫃
put ~ in the cupboard

把～放入冰箱（冷藏室）/ 冷凍庫（冷凍櫃）
put ~ in the refrigerator [fridge]/freezer

冷藏保管
keep ~ in the refrigerator, keep ~ refrigerated

冷凍保管
keep ~ in the freezer, keep ~ frozen

冷凍
freeze ~

解凍
defrost ~

把～從冰箱（冷藏室）/ 冷凍庫（冷凍櫃）取出
take ~ out of the refrigerator[fridge]/freezer

洗米
wash rice

把米泡水
soak rice in water

切除肉的油脂部位
trim the meat

洗蔬菜
wash vegetables

切除蔬菜末端、處理蔬菜
cut the ends off the vegetables, clean vegetables

SENTENCES TO USE

他立即把買回來的食物放進冰箱。
He immediately put the food he had bought in the refrigerator.

此產品必須冷凍保管。
This product needs to be kept frozen.

我把肉從冷藏室裡拿出來解凍。
I took the meat out of the freezer and defrosted it.

我洗好米並且將它泡水。
I washed the rice and soaked it in water.

我媽媽把從田裡採回來的蔬菜的末端切除。
My mother cut the ends off the vegetables she had gathered from the field.

處理魚
clean a fish
去除魚內臟
gut a fish

去除腐壞的部位
remove[cut out]
the rotten part

削皮、剝皮
peel

剪、切
cut

把～切塊、切片
cut ~ into
pieces

去除肉或魚的骨頭
fillet

剁碎
chop

切成條（絲）狀
julienne,
shred

切薄片
slice (thinly),
cut ~ into (thin) slices

切丁
dice, cube,
cut ~ into
cubes

切末、切碎肉
mince, finely chop

磨、搗
grind

在刨絲器上刨成絲狀或磨碎
grate

擠壓出汁液
squeeze

SENTENCES TO USE

處理魚很困難。
請把鯖魚切成兩塊。
放在飯捲裡的紅蘿蔔要切成細條。
請把要放入咖哩裡的馬鈴薯切丁。
我把肉剁碎，以便做餃子。
我用刨絲器刨薑，做了薑茶。

It's hard to clean a fish.
Cut the mackerel into two pieces, please.
You have to shred carrots for kimbap.
Cut the potatoes into cubes for the curry, please.
I minced the meat to make dumplings.
I made ginger tea by grating ginger with a grater.

029

煮飯、做飯
cook rice,
make rice

醃辛奇
make kimchi

用鹽醃漬
salt
鹽漬的
salted

醃（黃瓜、菜）
pickle
醃製的
pickled

以醬料醃泡
marinate
以醬料醃泡的
marinated

調味
season
調過味的
seasoned

蒸
steam

燒開、煮
boil

汆燙
blanch

小火燉煮
simmer

油炸、油煎
fry

（油覆蓋食材）油炸
deep-fry

SENTENCES TO USE

他有生以來第一次煮飯。 He cooked rice for the first time in his life.

醃辛奇沒有我想像中那麼困難。 Making kimchi wasn't as hard as I thought.

韓國人在料理排骨前會先醃過。 Koreans marinate ribs before cooking them.

我用大醬和芝麻油調味蔬菜。 I seasoned the vegetables with soybean paste and sesame oil.

將雞蛋用水煮15分鐘左右。 Boil the eggs for about 15 minutes.

你曾經油炸過整隻魷魚嗎？ Have you ever deep-fried a whole squid?

大火翻炒
stir-fry

翻面
flip

烘焙、烤（麵包）
bake

（在烤箱）烘烤
roast

（用烤架）燒烤
grill

烤整塊肉、用直火燒烤
barbecue

攪拌、攪勻
stir

拌勻、混合
mix

搗成泥狀
mash

（把雞蛋等）攪拌至起泡沫
whisk

SENTENCES TO USE

翻炒洋蔥、紅椒粉、香腸，再加入番茄醬提味。

要乾淨俐落地把韓式煎餅翻面不是一件容易的事。

你比較喜歡用烤箱烤的牛肉還是用烤架烤的牛肉？

把煮熟的馬鈴薯搗成泥狀後，
加入美乃滋、鹽巴和胡椒一起攪拌。

在雞蛋裡加入油和醋，攪拌一段時間後，
你就會得到美乃滋。

Stir-fry onion, paprika, and sausage and then add ketchup to taste.

It's not easy to flip a Korean style pancake neatly.

Which do you prefer, a roast or grilled beef?

Mash boiled potatoes and mix with ayonnaise, salt, and pepper.

Add oil and vinegar to the eggs and whisk for a while, and you will have mayonnaise.

傾倒
pour

撒
sprinkle

均勻塗抹（奶油、果醬等）
spread

打蛋
crack[break] an egg

用麵粉做麵團
make dough from flour

揉麵團
knead dough

使麵團發酵
let dough rise

壓平
flatten

使用餅乾模具
use a cookie cutter

SENTENCES TO USE

在義大利麵上撒些香芹粉很美觀。
那孩子生平第一次打蛋。
麵團必須揉大約30分鐘。
讓麵團發酵兩次，每次一小時。
我使用星形餅乾模具。

Sprinkling parsley powder over the pasta looks good.
The child broke an egg for the first time in her life.
You have to knead the dough for about 30 minutes.
Let the dough rise twice, an hour each time.
I used the star-shaped cookie cutter.

調小 / 調大爐火
turn down/up
the gas

切斷（關掉）瓦斯
shut[turn] off the gas

開 / 關瓦斯爐
turn on/off the gas stove

關 / 開瓦斯閥
close/open the gas valve

用電子鍋煮飯
cook rice in a rice cooker

用微波爐加熱～
heat ~ in the microwave

烤吐司
make toast

用烤箱烤麵包
bake bread in the oven

用烤箱烤肉
roast meat in the oven

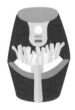

用氣炸鍋料理 / 做～
cook/make ~ in an air fryer

SENTENCES TO USE

當燉煮的菜開始沸騰時，要把爐火調小。

使用完瓦斯爐後，要關掉瓦斯閥。

食用前，在微波爐加熱一分鐘。

烤好吐司後，我在吐司上塗抹奶油和果醬，和咖啡一起享用。

你可以不使用任何油，用氣炸鍋做出油炸料理。

Turn down the gas when the stew starts to boil.

Close the gas valve after using the gas stove.

Heat it in the microwave for about 1 minute before eating.

After making toast, I spread butter and jam on it and had it with a cup of coffee.

You can make fried food without using any oil in an air fryer.

用水壺 / 電熱水壺燒開水
boil water in a kettle/
an electric kettle

用咖啡機煮咖啡
brew[make] coffee
with a coffee maker

在砧板上切～
cut ~ on a cutting
[chopping] board

用攪拌機攪拌～
blend ~
in a blender

用料理秤秤～
weigh ~ on[using]
the kitchen scale(s)

用篩子過濾～
strain ~
through a sieve

用抹布擦桌子
wipe the table
with a dishcloth

打開廚房抽油煙機
turn on the kitchen
[range] hood

把～放入洗碗機
put ~ in the
dishwasher,
load the dishwasher

打開洗碗機開關
turn on the
dishwasher

啟動洗碗機
run the
dishwasher

穿圍裙

（動作）
put on
an apron

（狀態）
wear
an apron

SENTENCES TO USE

請用電熱水壺煮些開水。   Please boil some water in an electric kettle.

她在砧板上切豆腐。   She cut tofu on the cutting board.

她用攪拌機打一些蔬菜和水果。   She blended some vegetables and fruits in a blender.

我用料理秤秤粉的重量。   I weighed the powder using the kitchen scale.

把碗放進洗碗機。   Put the bowls in the dishwasher.

4 吃東西、招待

吃飯
have a meal

吃早餐 / 午餐 / 晚餐
eat[have] breakfast/lunch/
supper[dinner]

吃點心
have[eat] a snack

吃～當作點心
eat ~ for a snack

吃消夜
have[eat] a late-night snack

吃～當作消夜
eat ~ for a late-night snack

將食物盛到盤子裡吃
put food on one's plate
and eat

與他人分享食物
share food with
others

供應食物
offer food

擺餐具
set the table

收拾餐桌
clear the table

以杓舀取
ladle ~

以飯勺盛飯
scoop rice with a rice paddle

SENTENCES TO USE

點心吃番茄、蘋果和牛奶。

我必須改掉吃消夜的習慣。

為了預防傳染病，
你應該把食物盛到自己的盤子裡再吃。

我差不多煮好了，請擺放餐具。

廚師們正在用杓子幫員工們舀湯。

Eat tomatoes, apples, and milk for snacks.

I have to break the habit of eating late-night snacks.

To prevent infectious diseases, you should
put food on your plate and then eat it.

I'm almost done cooking, so please set the table.

Cooks are ladling soup for the employees.

用湯匙舀～
spoon up ~,
scoop ~ with a spoon

用筷子夾～
pick up ~ with
chopsticks

用叉子叉取食物
pick up food
with a fork

使用湯匙 / 筷子 / 叉
子 / 刀子
use a spoon/
chopsticks/a fork/
a knife

用刀子切～
cut ~ with a knife

咀嚼
chew ~

來回咀嚼
chew on ~, keep chewing ~

吞嚥
swallow ~

喝湯
drink the soup

大口吞（喝下）～
gulp (down) ~

用生菜 / 紫蘇葉包肉吃
eat meat wrapped in
lettuce/perilla leaves

SENTENCES TO USE

我不太會使用筷子，所以很難用筷子夾起食物。

我右邊有顆臼齒很痛，無法用那邊咀嚼食物。

有些人有吞嚥困難。

在韓國，我們用生菜和紫蘇葉包肉吃。

I'm not good at using chopsticks, so it's hard
to pick up food with chopsticks.

One of my right molars hurts, so I can't chew
on that side.

Some people have difficulty swallowing.

In Korea, we eat meat wrapped in lettuce and
perilla leaves.

狼吞虎嚥地吃、貪婪大口地吞食
devour ~, eat greedily, gobble ~ up,
wolf ~ down, eat ~ in a hurry

挑食、小口小口吃
pick at ~,
nibble at ~

發出咀嚼聲（吃東西發出聲音）
eat noisily with one's mouth open,
lick[smack] one's lips while eating

強嚥下去
choke down ~

吐出
spit out ~

用餐巾擦嘴
wipe one's mouth
with a napkin

端上（食物）
serve ~

幫～打包（食物）
give ~ to take
home

SENTENCES TO USE

他餓到狼吞虎嚥地吃飯。

不要吃這麼小口，多吃一點。

那男子吃飯發出咀嚼的聲音，真令人反感。

如果食物不合胃口，我的貓會馬上把它吐出來。

每次去看我媽媽，她都會為我準備各種
小菜讓我打包回家。

He was so hungry that he ate his meal in a hurry.

Don't nibble at your food. Eat a lot.

The man eats noisily with his mouth open, and
that's annoying.

My cat spits out food right away if it doesn't suit
her taste.

My mom gives me various side dishes to take
home every time I go to see her.

CHAPTER

3

外食

EATING OUT

在咖啡廳

選擇要喝的飲料
choose drinks[beverages]
to drink

點飲料
order drinks
[beverages]

付飲料費
pay for
the drinks

用電子禮券購買飲料
buy a drink with
a mobile gift card
[mobile gift voucher]

用電子禮券兌換飲料
exchange a mobile
gift card[mobile gift
voucher] for a drink

掃電子禮券條碼
scan the
bar code
of a mobile gift card

在自助點餐機點餐
order from
a kiosk

確認電子螢幕的號碼
check the number on
the electronic display

取餐呼叫器響
a[the] pager
rings

領取點的飲料
pick up the drinks

在～加糖漿
add syrup to ~

SENTENCES TO USE

近來有很多咖啡廳要在櫃檯點飲料。
These days, there are many cafes where you have to order drinks at the counter.

現在仍然有坐在位置上向服務生點飲料的咖啡廳。
There are still cafes where you sit down and order drinks from the staff.

我用朋友送我的電子禮券買了一杯飲料。
I bought a drink with a mobile gift card from my friend.

當取餐呼叫器響的時候，你可以到櫃檯領取飲料。
When the pager rings, you can go to the counter and get the drinks.

點好飲料後，我領取我的飲料到我的座位上。
After ordering a drink, I pick up the drink I ordered and take it to the seat.

（在咖啡廳等場所）找座位
get a table

喝
drink ~

說話、聊天
talk,
have a chat

喝咖啡
over coffee

上廁所
use the bathroom

外帶～
buy ~ for takeout, order[get] ~ to go

掃描 QR codes
check in[register] with QR codes,
scan QR codes

歸還空的 / 使用過的杯子和托盤
return one's empty/
used cups and trays

SENTENCES TO USE

我們在咖啡廳喝咖啡聊天。

We chatted over coffee at the café.

為了上廁所，她去咖啡廳買了一杯飲料。

She went to a café and bought a drink to use the bathroom.

我外帶了一杯冰拿鐵咖啡。

I bought a glass of iced caffè latte for takeout.

現在進去一間咖啡廳時必須掃 QR code。

These days, you have to register with a QR code when entering a café.

當你離開那間咖啡廳時，必須歸還空杯和托盤。

You have to return your empty cups and trays when you leave the café.

預約～人座位
book[reserve] a table for ~ (people),
make a reservation for ~ (people)

排隊等候
wait in line

把名字登記在候位名單上
put one's name
on the waiting list

（在菜單上）選擇餐點
choose an item from the
menu, choose a dish

叫服務生過來
ask for[call, summon]
a server

（請別人）推薦菜單
ask for a
recommendation

要酒單
ask for
the wine list

點餐
order a meal

放湯匙、筷子在餐桌上
put spoons and
chopsticks on the table

倒一杯水
pour a glass of
water

SENTENCES TO USE

我打電話到餐廳訂了一張6人桌。
I called the restaurant and booked a table for six.

那家餐廳非常受歡迎，你必須排隊等候。
That restaurant is so popular that you have to wait in line.

餐廳把我的名字登記在候位名單上，
然後我等了大約半個小時。
I put my name on the waiting list at the restaurant and
waited for about half an hour.

對我來説，在餐廳點菜並不容易。
It's not easy for me to choose a dish at a restaurant.

等待餐點時，他在桌上擺放湯匙和筷子，
並倒了幾杯水。
Waiting for food, he put spoons and chopsticks on the
table and poured glasses of water.

烤肉

索取多的盤子 / 個人盤子（小盤子）
ask for extra/
individual plates

加點餐點
order more[extra]
food

（在烤箱）
roast meat

（在鐵網或烤架）
grill meat

把肉翻面
turn the meat over

用剪刀剪肉
cut meat with
(kitchen) scissors

切牛排
cut steak,
slice steak

用叉子捲起義大利麵
wrap spaghetti
around a fork

拍食物照
take pictures
[photos] of food

打翻食物
spill food

打翻水
spill water

在食物裡發現一根頭髮
find a hair
in the food

抱怨食物
complain
about food

SENTENCES TO USE

我們向餐廳員工索取小盤子。
在韓國，烤肉時會用剪刀剪開肉。
聽說我們應該用叉子捲起義大利麵吃。
很多人拍下食物的照片並上
傳到社群媒體。
我今天在餐廳吃飯，在食物裡發現了
一根頭髮。

We asked the restaurant worker for individual plates.
In Korea, when we grill meat, we cut the meat with scissors.
They say we should wrap the spaghetti around a fork to eat it.
Many people take pictures of food and post
them on SNS.
I was eating at the restaurant today and found a hair in
the food.

把剩菜打包帶回家
pack the leftovers and
take/bring them home

上廁所
use the bathroom

索取帳單
ask for the bill

買單、付餐費
pay the bill,
pay for the meal

各付各的
go Dutch

各付一半
pay half and half,
pay fifty-fifty

平均分攤
split the bill

掃描 QR codes
check in[register] with
QR codes, scan QR codes

外帶～
order ~ for takeout,
order[get] ~ to go

電話訂餐
order food
by phone

用外送應用程式訂餐
order food through
a (food) delivery app

SENTENCES TO USE

我把餐廳裡的剩菜打包帶回家。
I packed the leftovers from the restaurant and brought them home.
那家餐廳的餐費必須事先支付。
We have to pay for the meal in advance at the restaurant.
我和朋友們見面用餐時，都是平均分攤帳單。
When I meet my friends and have a meal, we split the bill.
我多點一份同樣的餐點，要外帶給我媽媽。
I ordered one more of the same dish for takeout for my mom.
現在很多人用外送應用程式點餐。
Many people order food through delivery apps these days.

I BOUGHT a glass of iced caffè latte
FOR TAKEOUT.

CHAPTER

4

住家

HOUSE

場所別 ① - 臥室

034

就寢
go to bed,
go to sleep

（對旁邊的人）道晚安
say good night to ~

鬧鐘設定～點
set the alarm for ~

戴上（睡眠用）眼罩
wear
a sleep mask

輾轉反側
toss and turn

睡著
fall asleep

睡覺
sleep

仰睡
sleep on
one's back

側睡
sleep on
one's side

睡覺時翻身
turn over
in one's sleep

說夢話
talk in one's sleep

打呼
snore

睡覺時磨牙
grind one's teeth
in one's sleep

SENTENCES TO USE

明天我必須一早出發，
所以我把鬧鐘設定在5點。

I set the alarm for 5 o'clock because
I have to leave early tomorrow.

我通常側躺著睡覺。

I usually sleep on my side.

你昨晚說夢話。

You were talking in your sleep last night.

我的丈夫打呼很大聲。

My husband snores loudly.

我的弟弟會在睡覺時磨牙。

My brother grinds his teeth in his sleep.

整理床鋪
make one's bed

鋪被褥在地板上
spread the[one's]
bedding on the floor

疊起被褥
fold up the
bedding

蓋棉被
cover oneself
with bedclothes
[blanket]

（睡覺時）踢棉被
kick the
blanket out
(while sleeping)

更換床單
change the bed,
change the
sheets

更換枕頭套
change the
pillowcase

醒來
wake up

起床
get up,
get out of bed

（睡覺時）
從床上掉下來
fall[roll] off the bed
while sleeping

關掉鬧鐘
turn off
the alarm

伸懶腰
stretch (one's body)

打哈欠
yawn

穿 / 脫睡衣
put on/take off
one's pajamas

穿
put on ~

SENTENCES TO USE

你應該每天整理床鋪。　　　　You should make your bed every day.

我的祖母把被褥鋪在地上睡覺。　My grandmother spread her bedding on the floor to
go to sleep.

你多久更換枕頭套？　　　　　How often do you change the pillowcase?

她從床上起床，伸了個懶腰。　She got out of bed and stretched.

他脫掉睡衣，穿上衣服。　　　He took off his pajamas and put on his clothes.

035

休息
relax,
take[have] a rest

躺在沙發上
lie on the sofa[couch]

看窗外
look out (of) the window

看書
read a book

畫畫
draw[paint] a picture

彈鋼琴 / 吉他
play the piano/guitar

SENTENCES TO USE

下班後，她在客廳看電視休息。
After work, she relaxes by watching TV in the living room.

我上週日整天躺在沙發上看電視。
Last Sunday, I lay on the sofa watching TV all day long.

我的貓喜歡坐在貓跳台，從客廳的窗戶往外看。
My cat likes to sit on the cat tree and look out the living room window.

他週末會在書房裡看書或畫畫。
He reads books or draws pictures in the study on weekends.

做徒手運動
do free-hand exercises

做瑜伽
do[practice] yoga

上網
surf the Internet

在電腦 / 筆記型電腦上打字
write on
a computer/laptop

玩社群媒體、在～留言 / 上傳圖片
spend time on social media,
post comments/pictures on
＋特定社群媒體名稱

看電視 / 電影 / Netflix / YouTube 影片
watch TV/a movie/Netflix/YouTube (videos)

SENTENCES TO USE

我每天在客廳做徒手運動。
I do free-hand exercises in the living room every day.

我會在書房裡上網或看 Netflix 來消磨時間。
I spend my time surfing the Internet or watching Netflix in my study.

她每天花好幾個小時在社群媒體上。
She spends several hours on social media every day.

他下班後邊吃飯邊看 YouTube 影片。
He watches YouTube videos while having dinner after work.

036

料理、做～（菜餚）
cook, make[cook] ~

烤麵包
bake bread

煮咖啡
brew coffee, make coffee

做午餐便當
pack a lunch (box)

擺餐具
set the table

吃
eat ~

吃早餐 / 午餐 / 晚餐
eat[have] breakfast/
lunch/supper[dinner]

收拾餐桌
clear the table

洗碗
wash[do] the dishes

SENTENCES TO USE

我不久前開始烤麵包。
她早上起床後的第一件事是去煮咖啡。
最近我每天早上都準備午餐便當。
你用餐結束後應該要馬上洗碗。

I started baking bread a while ago.
When she wakes up in the morning, she makes coffee first.
These days, I pack a lunch every morning.
After finishing the meal, you should wash the dishes right away.

打開洗碗機開關
turn on the dishwasher

把碗盤放入洗碗機
load[stack] a dishwasher

啟動洗碗機
run the dishwasher

整理、清潔冰箱
clean the[one's]
refrigerator

處理廚餘
dispose of food waste

打開廚房抽油煙機
turn on the kitchen[range] hood

SENTENCES TO USE

我做飯，我的丈夫整理
餐桌和使用洗碗機。

你應該要定期清潔冰箱。

處理廚餘比洗碗更麻煩。

做菜的時候要打開廚房抽油煙機。

I cook, and my husband clears the table and runs the dishwasher.

You have to clean your refrigerator regularly.

Disposing of food waste is more of a hassle than washing dishes.

Turn on the kitchen hood when you cook.

4 場所別 ④ - 浴室

 037

洗手
wash one's hands

洗臉
wash one's face

刷牙
brush one's teeth

使用牙線
floss (one's teeth), use dental floss

使用牙間刷
use an interdental (tooth)brush

刮鬍子
shave

洗頭
wash one's hair

吹乾頭髮
dry one's hair

梳頭髮
comb[brush] one's hair

（自己）做頭髮
do one's hair

淋浴
take[have] a shower

泡澡
take[have] a bath

在浴缸放洗澡水
fill the bathtub

擦化妝水 / 乳液 / 乳霜
apply[put] toner/lotion/cream
(on one's face)

擦身體乳
apply[put] body lotion
(on one's body)

SENTENCES TO USE

外出回來後要馬上洗手。	You should wash your hands as soon as you get back.
使用牙線或牙間刷。	Floss or use an interdental toothbrush.
晚上洗頭比較好。	It's better to wash your hair at night.
邦妮有個約會，所以她做了頭髮。	Bonnie had a date, so she did her hair.
用溫水淋浴比較好。	It's better to take showers with lukewarm water.
如果你的皮膚乾燥，一定要擦身體乳液。	If your skin is dry, make sure to apply body lotion.

剪手指甲／腳趾甲
cut[clip] one's
nails/toenails

染頭髮
dye one's hair

化妝
put on makeup

卸妝
remove (one's)
makeup

小便
go to the bathroom, pee（兒童用語）,
do[go, make] number one,
urinate（醫療、生物學用語）

大便
go to the bathroom,
poop（兒童用語）, do[go, make]
number two, defecate（醫療、
生物學用語）

使用免治馬桶
use a bidet

沖馬桶
flush
the toilet

疏通馬桶
unclog
a toilet

清潔浴室
clean
the bathroom

清洗浴缸
clean
the (bath)tub

換上新的捲筒衛生紙
put a new roll of
paper in the holder

SENTENCES TO USE

我把指甲剪得太短。
I cut my nails too short.

他把頭髮染成藍色。
He dyed his hair blue.

有句話説：卸妝比化妝重要。
There is a saying that it is more important to
remove makeup than to put on makeup.

有些人上公共廁所忘記沖馬桶。
There are people who forget to flush the
toilet in public restrooms.

如果你不每週打掃廁所至少一到兩次，就會發霉。
If you don't clean the bathroom at least once
or twice a week, you'll get mold.

5 場所別 ⑤ - 洗衣間、陽台、倉庫

洗衣服
wash the clothes,
do the laundry

用洗衣機洗衣服
do the laundry
using the
washing machine

分類待洗衣物
sort the laundry

把白色衣服和有色衣服分開
separate the colors from
the whites

把待洗衣物放入洗衣機
load the washing machine,
put the laundry in the
washing machine

加入洗衣劑 / 衣物柔軟精
add detergent/fabric
softener

取出洗好的衣物
unload the washing machine,
take the laundry out of the
washing machine

（在曬衣架、晾衣繩上）晾衣服
hang (out) the laundry
(on a clothes drying rack/clothesline)

收曬好的衣服
get the laundry,
take the laundry off the clothesline

啟動烘衣機
run a clothes
dryer

清洗洗衣槽
clean the washing
machine tub

SENTENCES TO USE

洗衣機讓洗衣服變得很輕鬆。

The washing machine made it really easy to do the laundry.

你要把白色衣服和有色衣服分開後再洗。

You have to separate the colors from the whites and then wash it.

洗衣流程結束後，請把洗好的衣物從洗衣機裡拿出來。

Please take the laundry out of the washing machine when the cycle is finished.

下雨了，於是我把衣服晾在房裡的曬衣架上。

It rained, so I hung out the laundry on the clothes drying rack in the room.

開始下雨了，於是我把院子裡晾衣繩上的衣服收進來。

It started to rain, so I took the laundry off the clothesline in the yard.

種植物 / 花 / 蔬菜
grow plants/
flowers/
vegetables

替植物 / 花 / 蔬菜澆水
water the plants/
flowers/vegetables

用清水清洗陽台
clean the balcony
with water

把陽台裝飾成咖啡館
decorate the balcony like a cafe,
make the balcony as a coffee nook

＊ veranda? balcony?

韓國公寓或別墅裡被稱為「veranda
（遊廊、陽台）」的空間大部分其實應該
稱為「balcony（陽台）」會更適當，因
為 balcony 是指二樓以上建築物外側多
出來的空間；veranda 是指位於建築物
一樓外側，上有屋頂的平臺。

把東西存放在儲藏室
store things in the
storage room

放～在儲藏室
put ~ in the storage room
堆放～在儲藏室
pile ~ up in the storage room
從儲藏室拿出～
take ~ out of the storage room

SENTENCES TO USE

我媽媽在陽台種了許多植物和花。
今年我要在陽台上種蔬菜。
我今天用清水打掃陽台。
我們在儲藏室存放了不使用的物品、
電風扇、衛生紙等等。
把吸塵器放在儲藏室。

My mom grows many plants and flowers on the balcony.
I'm going to grow vegetables on the balcony this year.
I cleaned the balcony with water today.
We store unused items, electric fans, tissues, etc. in the storage room.
Put the vacuum in the storage room.

039

| 停車
park,
park a car | 把車子從停車場開走
take the car out of
the parking lot | 開啟 / 關閉車庫門
open/close
the garage door | 手工洗車
hand-wash
one's car | 辦烤肉派對
have a barbecue
(party) |

| 栽種樹木 / 花朵
plant/grow
trees/flowers | 在菜園裡種植蔬菜
grow vegetables in the
vegetable[kitchen] garden | 替植物 / 花 / 蔬菜澆水
water the plants/
flowers/vegetables | 替菜園施肥
fertilize the
vegetable garden |

| 採、摘蔬菜
pick (the)
vegetables | 在院子裡造景布置
do landscaping
work in the yard | 幫花園鋪上草皮
turf the garden,
lay the garden
with turf | 修剪草坪
mow
the lawn | 拔雜草
weed,
pull (up) weeds |

SENTENCES TO USE

他在家裡自己洗他的車子。	He hand-washes his car himself at home.
上週六我在頂樓和朋友們舉辦烤肉派對。	I had a barbecue party with my friends on the rooftop last Saturday.
莫妮卡在菜園裡栽種各種蔬菜。	Monica grows various vegetables in the vegetable garden.
最近都沒下雨， 所以我必須幫菜園裡的蔬菜澆水。	It hasn't rained lately, so I have to water the vegetables in the kitchen garden.
我摘自家菜園裡的蔬菜來做沙拉。	I pick vegetables in the kitchen garden and make a salad.

040

住家清潔

打掃房子
clean
the house

用吸塵器吸地板、用吸塵器
vacuum the floor,
run the vacuum cleaner

給吸塵器充電
charge the
vacuum cleaner

用掃把掃
sweep ~

用耙子掃樹葉
rake (the)
leaves

用拖把拖地
mop the floor,
run a mop over the floor

用（濕）抹布擦
wipe ~ with a rag
[with wet cloth]

洗拖把（抹布）
wash
a mop[rag]

用黏毛滾輪清除寵物毛髮
remove pet hair with
a lint roller

擦窗框的灰塵
wipe the dust off
the window frames

清潔浴室
clean the
bathroom

整理壁櫥 / 抽屜
organize[clean out]
one's closet/drawer

整理鞋架（鞋櫃）
arrange
one's shoe rack
[shoe closet]

SENTENCES TO USE

我必須每兩天用吸塵器吸地板一次。

他用耙子把院子裡的落葉掃成堆。

你得拖地才行。

用抹布擦桌子和書桌。

我必須不停地用黏毛滾輪清除我家貓咪的貓毛。

I have to vacuum the floor once every other day.

He raked the leaves in the yard.

You have to mop the floor.

Wipe the table and desk with a rag.

I have to keep removing my cat's hair with a lint roller.

清空垃圾桶
empty the
waste basket
[trash can]

分類垃圾
sort garbage
[waste]

把垃圾 / 可回收垃圾
拿出去丟
take out the garbage
[waste]/recyclables

將可回收垃圾與一般垃圾分類
separate the recyclables
and the trash, sort the
recyclables

其他家務

規劃一週菜單
plan a week's
meals

列出購物清單
make a grocery list

購物
do (the, one's) shopping

購買食品雜貨
do grocery shopping

熨燙
iron ~

照顧寵物
take care of pets

SENTENCES TO USE

把你房間的垃圾桶清空。
Empty the waste basket in your room.

垃圾必須依照一般垃圾、
廚餘、可回收垃圾來分類。
Garbage should be sorted as general waste, food waste, and recyclables.

在我的公寓大樓，我們必須在週五
把可回收垃圾拿出去丟。
In my apartment building, we have to take out the recyclables on Fridays.

列出購物清單可以節省你的時間，
並幫助你避免購買不必要的物品。
Making a grocery list saves you time and helps you avoid buying things unnecessarily.

我在下班的路上去採買食品雜貨。
I did grocery shopping on my way home from work.

熨燙襯衫和女性襯衫是最耗時的家事。
Ironing shirts and blouses is the most time-consuming chore.

8 家電用品使用

安裝
install ~

開 / 關電燈
turn on/off the light

開 / 關電腦 / 筆記型電腦
turn on/off the
computer/laptop

開 / 關電視
turn on/off
the TV

轉到~頻道
change
the channel to ~

把電視音量調大 / 調小
turn up/down
the TV (volume)

開 / 關冰箱門
open/close the
refrigerator (door)

調節冰箱溫度
adjust[control]
the temperature
on the refrigerator

開 / 關電磁爐
turn[switch] on/off
the induction
cooktop[stove]

調節電磁爐溫度
adjust[control] the
temperature on the induction
cooktop[stove]

開 / 關廚房抽油煙機
turn[switch] on/off the
kitchen[range] hood

SENTENCES TO USE

把不要用的燈關掉。	Turn off the lights you don't need.
轉到別的頻道。	Change the channel.
請把電視音量調小。	Please turn down the TV volume.
我必須調節一下冰箱的溫度。	I need to adjust the temperature on the refrigerator.
我不知道怎麼開電磁爐。	I don't know how to turn on the induction cooktop.

用微波爐加熱～
heat ~ in the microwave

從濾淨飲水機取水
get water from a water purifier

用電熱水壺煮水
boil water in an electric kettle

用氣炸鍋料理
cook[make] ~ in[with] an air fryer

冷氣開強（增溫）
turn up the air conditioner

冷氣調弱（降溫）
turn down the air conditioner

開／關冷氣
turn on/off the air conditioner

開／關電風扇
turn[switch] on/off the electric fan

供暖鍋爐／暖氣機開強（增溫）
turn up the boiler/heater

供暖鍋爐／暖氣機調弱（降溫）
turn down the boiler/heater

開／關供暖鍋爐／暖氣機
turn on/off the boiler/heater

SENTENCES TO USE

用微波爐將它加熱約4分鐘。 Heat it in the microwave for about 4 minutes.
你有用氣炸鍋炸過炸物嗎？ Have you ever made fried food in an air fryer?
好熱。請把冷氣開強一點。 It's too hot. Please turn up the air conditioner.
打開供暖鍋爐的季節就要到了。 The season to turn on the boiler is coming.
室內好熱。請把暖氣機溫度調低一點。 It's hot in here. Please turn down the heater.

打開 / 關閉加濕器
turn on/off the
humidifier

打開 / 關閉除濕機
turn on/off the
dehumidifier

打開 / 關閉空氣清淨機
turn on/off the
air purifier

用吹風機吹乾頭髮
dry one's hair with
a hair dryer

租
rent ~

打電話申請售後（維修）服務
call the after-sales service[customer
service] number (to get[have] ~ fixed)

接受～的售後服務
have ~ serviced

請人維修～
have[get] ~ fixed

安排別人來回收廢舊電器
arrange to have an old
appliance picked up

SENTENCES TO USE

冬天的房間很乾燥，我必須打開加濕器。
In winter, the room is dry, so I have to turn on the humidifier.

做好飯菜後，房間應通風換氣再打開空氣清淨機。
After cooking, you should turn on the air purifier after airing out the room.

最近也有很多人租用濾淨飲水機和空氣清淨機等家電產品。
Nowadays, many people rent home appliances such as water purifiers and air purifiers.

冰箱出了問題，所以我打電話申請售後服務。
There was a problem with the refrigerator, so I called the after-sales service number.

我已經安排別人來回收我的舊洗衣機。
I have arranged to have my old washing machine picked up.

🎧 042

整修、翻新房子
repair[renovate] the[one's] house

改造、改建房子
remodel the[one's] house

重新裝修房子
（貼壁紙、粉刷等）
redecorate the[one's] house

拿到房子維修報價單
get an estimate
for home repairs

拆除陽台／擴建客廳
remove[get rid of] the balcony/
widen the living room

在陽台舖設人工草皮
install artificial grass[turf]
on the balcony

SENTENCES TO USE

今年春天我打算整修我的房子。
聽説他改建他的房子之後把它賣掉了。
我的房子老舊了，我必須重新裝潢它。
那個公寓拆除了陽台，所以客廳很寬敞，
但是我喜歡有陽台的公寓。

I'm going to renovate my house this spring.
They say he remodeled and then sold his house.
My house is old, so I have to redecorate it.
The apartment has a large living room because
the balcony was removed, but I like an
apartment with a balcony.

住家裝設隔熱設計
insulate a house

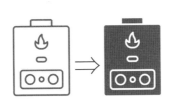

更換供暖鍋爐
replace the boiler

施作頂樓 / 屋頂防水工程
waterproof the rooftop/roof

重新鋪地板
redo the floor, lay a new floor

（房間）貼新壁紙
put up new wallpaper (in a room)

SENTENCES TO USE

我家供暖鍋爐壞了，必須換一個。

在經過十年後，我們重新施作屋頂防水工程。

你想重鋪地板嗎？木地板如何？

我們在搬進去以前將壁紙換新了。

My boiler is broken, so I have to replace it.

We waterproofed the rooftop again after 10 years.

Do you want to redo the floor? How about wood flooring?

We put up new wallpaper before we moved in.

鋪上新油氈地板
lay new linoleum

裝設壁爐
install a fireplace

更換水管
replace water pipes

更換窗框
replace window frames

重鋪浴室磁磚
retile the bathroom

安裝浴缸
install a bathtub

拆除浴缸，安裝淋浴間
remove a bathtub and
install a shower stall

更換蓮蓬頭
change[replace]
a shower head

除霉
remove[get rid of]
mold

SENTENCES TO USE

父母家裡的窗框已經老舊，我就把它們換了。

我想在浴室裝浴缸。

你可以使用這個清潔劑去除浴室磁磚上的霉。

I had the window frames of my parents' house replaced because they were old.

I want to install a bathtub in the bathroom.

You can remove mold from bathroom tiles with this detergent.

更換鏡子
change[replace] a mirror

更換燈泡
change[replace] a light bulb

更換成 LED 燈
switch to LED lights

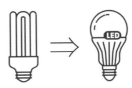

把日光燈換成 LED 燈
replace fluorescent lights with LED lights,
change fluorescent lights to LED lights

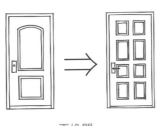

更換門
replace a door

更換門把
replace a doorknob

SENTENCES TO USE

我可以自己更換燈泡。 — I can change the light bulb myself.

曾經興起了把日光燈換成 LED 燈的熱潮。 — There was a boom in replacing fluorescent lights with LED lights.

我房門的門把壞了，所以我把它換了。 — The doorknob of my room was broken, so I replaced it.

CHAPTER

5

健康與疾病

HEALTH & DISEASE

流淚
shed tears

眼睛有眼屎
have[get] some
sleep[sand, gunk]
in one's eyes

打哈欠
yawn

肚子咕嚕咕嚕地叫
one's stomach growls

打嗝
hiccup

咳嗽
cough

打噴嚏
sneeze

打飽嗝
burp, belch

放屁
fart, pass gas

流汗
sweat

冒冷汗
break out into
a cold sweat

流鼻涕
have a runny nose,
one's nose runs

SENTENCES TO USE

我早上起床時，眼睛裡有很多眼屎。

I have a lot of gunk in my eyes when I wake up in the morning.

當你偏頭痛時，可能會經常打哈欠。
When you have a migraine, you might yawn a lot.

他因為過敏而一直打噴嚏。
He keeps sneezing because of allergies.

在與他人一起用餐時打嗝是不禮貌的。
It's not polite to burp while eating with others.

她自從進入更年期後就一直出汗。
She's been sweating a lot since she reached menopause.

小便
go to the bathroom, pee
（兒童用語）, do[go, make]
number one, urinate（醫療、
生物學用語）

大便
go to the bathroom, poop
（兒童用語）, do[go, make]
number two, defecate（醫療、
生物學用語）

生理期期間
have a period,
be on one's period

生理痛
have cramps,
have menstrual
[period] pain

飽受經前症候群的折磨
suffer from PMS
(premenstrual syndrome)

血壓上升
one's blood
pressure rises

血壓下降
one's blood
pressure goes down

感到口渴
feel[be]
thirsty

感到昏昏欲睡
feel[be]
drowsy

幾乎睏到要睡著
nearly fall
asleep

睏到閉上眼睛
be so sleepy one can't
keep one's eyes open

SENTENCES TO USE

媽媽，我要去尿尿。
我生理期來了，身體不太舒服。
我妹妹有嚴重經痛。
我頭痛時，血壓就會下降。
我昨晚幾乎沒睡，現在睏到快睡著了。

Mom, I'm going to pee.
I'm not feeling well because I'm on my period.
My sister has severe menstrual pain.
My blood pressure goes down when I get a headache.
I hardly slept last night, so I'm nearly falling asleep.

生病 be sick, be ill	～痛 ~ hurt(s) （身體部位）～疼痛 have a pain in ~	忍受疼痛 bear [tolerate] the pain	頭痛 / 肚子痛 / 背痛 / 牙痛 / 生理痛 have a headache/a stomachache/ a backache/a toothache/menstrual pain[period pain, menstrual cramps]

肩膀痠痛、僵硬
one's shoulders are stiff, have stiff
shoulders, feel stiff in the shoulders

喉嚨痛
have a sore throat

頸部痠痛、僵硬
one's neck is stiff

眼睛刺痛
one's eyes
smart[sting]

眼睛搔癢
one's eyes are
itchy

鼻塞
have a stuffy[stuffed]
nose, one's nose is
stuffed up[stuffy]

嘴唇乾裂、破皮
one's lips are[get]
chapped

SENTENCES TO USE

我的腳很痛，因為我走了好幾個小時。

他從昨晚開始就牙痛。

由於在筆記型電腦前長時間工作，
我的肩膀痠痛。

因為過敏的關係，我的眼睛很癢。

由於冬天天氣乾燥，我的嘴唇很容易乾裂。

My feet hurt because I walked for hours.

He has had a toothache since last night.

My shoulders are stiff because
I worked in front of my laptop for a long time.

My eyes are itchy because of allergies.

My lips get chapped easily in winter because
the weather is dry.

（手、腳）發麻
be numb, go numb

腿 / 關節 / 膝蓋痠痛
one's leg/joint/knee is sore,
one's leg/joint/knee aches

腿發麻
have pins and needles in one's leg,
one's leg is numb, have no feelings in one's leg,
one's leg falls asleep

吃藥　　　　　　吃～藥
take medicine　　take ~ medicine

服用藥丸 / 藥水 / 藥粉
take a pill[tablet]/liquid medicine/
powdered medicine

服用止痛藥 / 感冒藥 / 消化藥 / 抗生素 / 安眠藥
take a painkiller/cold medicine/
digestant[digestive medicine]/
antibiotics/a sleeping pill

SENTENCES TO USE

我的祖母說只要一下雨，她的膝蓋就會痠痛。

她因為生理痛而吃藥。

這孩子不太會吃藥粉。

他經常吃止痛藥，因為他有慢性頭痛。

My grandmother says her knees ache when it rains.

She took medicine because she had menstrual pain.

The child has difficulty taking powdered medicine.

He often takes painkillers because of his
chronic headaches.

~受傷
get hurt on ~,
hurt ~, injure ~

~在流血
~ is bleeding

膝蓋擦傷
scrape one's knee,
have one's knee skinned[scraped]

~接受治療
have one's ~ treated,
be treated for ~,
get treatment for ~

消毒傷口
disinfect a wound

在~擦軟膏
apply ointment[salve] to ~,
put[rub in] ointment[salve] on ~

在~貼 OK 繃
apply a Band-Aid to ~,
put a Band-Aid on ~

SENTENCES TO USE

那男子在騎腳踏車時摔倒，腿受了傷。 The man fell while riding a bicycle and hurt his leg.

我弟弟跌倒，擦破了膝蓋。 My brother fell and scraped his knee.

她一直在接受背痛的治療。 She has been getting ongoing treatment for back pain.

他在傷口上擦軟膏，並且貼上 OK 繃。 He applied ointment to the wound and put a Band-Aid on it.

用繃帶包紮～
apply[put]
a bandage to ~

在～打石膏
wear[apply] a cast
to[on] ~

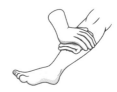

止血
stop the bleeding

冰敷
cool ~, put an ice[a cold] pack on ~

熱敷
put a hot pack on ~

針灸
get acupuncture

做指壓
get acupressure

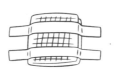

用紗布蓋住傷口
cover the wound with
a piece of gauze

把膿從～擠出來
squeeze the pus
from[out of] ~

SENTENCES TO USE

她腳踝骨折，打了石膏。
傷口一直流血，我必須止血。
在腫脹的部位冰敷是很好的。
我的祖母背痛時就會去針灸。

She broke her ankle and wore a cast.
The wound kept bleeding, so I had to stop the bleeding.
It's good to put cold packs on swollen areas.
My grandmother gets acupuncture when her back hurts.

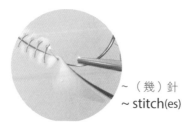

~（幾）針
~ stitch(es)

把～的結痂摳下來
pick the scab from ~

縫合傷口
suture a wound

留下疤痕
have a scar,
a scar is left

扭傷手腕／腳踝
sprain one's
wrist/ankle

骨折
break a bone,
~ bone is broken

接受急救
receive first aid (treatment),
receive emergency treatment

幫～做人工呼吸
give someone
mouth-to-mouth

實施心肺復甦術
do CPR
(cardiopulmonary resuscitation)

SENTENCES TO USE

那孩子跌倒並劃傷額頭，需要縫10針。
The child fell and cut his forehead, and required 10 stitches.

我的膝蓋有個小時候跌倒時留下的疤痕。
I have a scar on my knee that I got as a child from falling down.

那老人在冰面上滑倒，摔傷了臀部。
The old man slipped and fell on the ice and broke his hip.

我幫在地鐵昏倒的人做人工呼吸。
I gave mouth-to-mouth to the person who collapsed on the subway.

3 醫院 – 診療、檢查

跟醫生預約看診時間
make[schedule] an appointment with a doctor

接受診療
go see a doctor
接受治療
get medical treatment

量體溫
take[check] one's temperature

量血壓
take[check] one's blood pressure

量脈搏
take[check] one's pulse

抽血
have[get] blood taken

做血液檢查
take[have, get] a blood test

做尿液檢查
take[have, get] a urine test

做 X 光檢查
take[have, get] an X-ray

SENTENCES TO USE

當你覺得不舒服時，請去看醫生。
When you're not feeling well, go see a doctor.

自從他開始吃高血壓藥後，他每天都量血壓。
He has checked his blood pressure every day since he started taking high blood pressure pills.

我量了我的脈搏，它每分鐘跳動達90次。
I took my pulse, and it reached 90 beats a minute.

今天我在醫院做了血液和 X 光檢查。
I had a blood test and an X-ray at the hospital today.

做超音波檢查
take[have, get] an ultrasound

做腹部 / 乳房超音波檢查
take[have, get] an abdominal/a breast ultrasound

做乳房 X 光攝影檢查
get a mammogram

做子宮頸抹片檢查
get a Pap smear test

做心電圖檢查
take[have, get] an
ECG(electrocardiogram)

SENTENCES TO USE

我一年做一次乳房超音波檢查。
I take a breast ultrasound once a year.

當我做乳房X光攝影檢查時，我覺得乳房有點痛。
When I get a mammogram, I feel some pain in my breast.

我今天在醫院做了心電圖檢查，也檢查了我的心律調節器。
I had an ECG and had my pacemaker checked at the hospital today.

做電腦斷層攝影
have[get, do]
a CT scan

做核磁共振
造影檢查
have[get, do]
an MRI

做胃鏡 / 大腸鏡檢查
have[get] a
gastroscopy/
colonoscopy

切除息肉
have a polyp
removed

做～切片檢查
have[get, take]
a ~ biopsy

做糞便檢查
have[get]
scatoscopy

做 B 型肝炎檢查
get tested for
hepatitis B

做口腔檢查
get a dental
checkup

做視力 / 聽力檢查
have one's eyesight/
hearing tested

被診斷出患有～
be diagnosed
with ~

拿到～的處方箋
be prescribed ~

打針
get a shot,
get an injection

打～預防針、打～疫苗
get vaccinated
against ~

做定期檢查
have[get]
a regular
checkup

SENTENCES TO USE

他經常頭痛，所以做了腦部核磁共振造影檢查。	He had a brain MRI because he often had headaches.
你應該至少每兩年做一次胃鏡檢查。	You should get a gastroscopy at least once every two years.
去年我做了乳房切片檢查，幸好檢查結果不是癌症。	I had a breast biopsy last year, but fortunately it came back negative for cancer.
他在40歲出頭時被診斷出患有高血壓。	He was diagnosed with high blood pressure in his early forties.
昨天我接種了新冠肺炎疫苗。	I got vaccinated against COVID-19 yesterday.

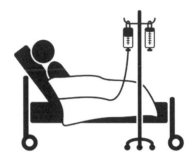

住院
be hospitalized,
be admitted to (the) hospital

住院中
be in the hospital

辦理住院手續
go through the hospitalization process

排定手術日期
schedule surgery[an operation],
set a date and time for surgery[an operation]

簽署手術同意書
sign the surgery consent form

聽手術前注意事項
listen to the precautions before surgery

（～期間）禁食
fast (for ~)

移動到手術室
be taken to the operating room

SENTENCES TO USE

他住院接受化療。　　　　　He was hospitalized for chemotherapy.
我的母親安排了心臟瓣膜手術。　My mother scheduled a heart valve operation.
手術前你必須禁食12小時。　　You have to fast for 12 hours before surgery.

被麻醉
be anesthetized

從麻醉中清醒
wake up from anesthesia

做～手術
have[get] ~ surgery
[a(n) ~ operation]

做開腹手術 / 開胸手術
have[get] an open abdominal/
open chest surgery

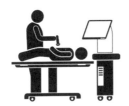

做腹腔鏡 / 內視鏡手術
have[get] laparoscopic/
endoscopic surgery

* surgery 和 operation

surgery：以抽象概念表達「手術」，一般作為不可數名詞。
operation：表示一次一次的手術，是可數名詞。

SENTENCES TO USE

手術後，我在恢復室從麻醉中清醒過來。

I woke up from anesthesia in the recovery room after the surgery.

她去年春天做了胃癌手術。

She had gastric cancer surgery last spring.

如果你做腹腔鏡手術，
會比開腹手術恢復得更快。

If you have laparoscopic surgery, you will recover faster than if you have an open abdominal surgery.

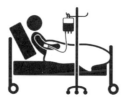

接受輸血
have[get, receive,
be given] a blood transfusion

手術後移動至恢復室 / 一般病房
be taken to the recovery room/
general ward after surgery

從～手術後恢復
recover from ~ surgery
[a(n) ~ operation]

陷入昏迷狀態
fall into a coma

手術後拆線
have stitches removed
after surgery

手術後排氣
fart[pass gas,
break wind] after surgery

SENTENCES TO USE

那病人在手術過程中需要輸血。
他做了痔瘡手術，正在恢復中。
很不幸地，那病人在手術中陷入昏迷。
術後排氣是個好徵兆。

The patient had to get a blood transfusion during surgery.
He's recovering from a hemorrhoids operation.
Unfortunately, the patient fell into a coma during surgery.
It's a good sign when you pass gas after some surgeries.

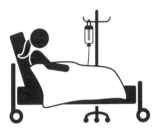

打點滴
get an IV (injection[shot]),
get an intravenous shot

吃藥、吃～藥
take medicine,
take a(n) ~ pill

辦理出院手續
go through the discharge
procedure

出院
be discharged
(from (the) hospital),
leave (the) hospital

領取提交給保險公司的單據
be issued documents
to submit to the insurance company

預約下次看診
schedule a doctor's
appointment

SENTENCES TO USE

我在住院期間都打點滴。

那病人每天三餐飯後服藥。

她住院兩個月後，在昨天出院了。

當她出院時，
她領取了提交給保險公司的單據。

I got IV injections throughout my hospital stay.

The patient is taking medicine three times a day after meals.

She was discharged yesterday after two months in the hospital.

When she was discharged from the hospital, she was
issued documents to submit to the insurance company.

開始節食、減肥
go on a diet

減肥、節食
be on a diet

減重
lose weight

規劃減肥食譜
plan a diet

吃得少
eat little, eat like a bird

不吃晚餐
skip dinner

一天吃一餐
eat one meal a day

進行一天一餐斷食
be on an OMAD diet

得厭食症
get anorexia, suffer from anorexia, be anorexic

進行低碳高脂飲食
be on an LCHF
(low carbohydrate high fat) diet

進行單一飲食減重
be on a mono diet, be on a single-food diet

進行間歇性斷食
be on an intermittent diet

用中藥減肥
lose weight with herbal medicine

SENTENCES TO USE

那位女演員一整年都在節食。　The actress is on a diet all year round.

她總是說自己需要減重。　She always says she needs to lose weight.

據說他一年多來都一天只吃一餐。　He is said to have been eating one meal a day for more than a year.

執行低碳高脂飲食的人不在少數。　More than a few people are on an LCHF diet.

我不認為單一飲食減重對你的健康有益。　I don't think a single-food diet is good for your health.

服用食慾抑制劑
take an appetite suppressant

做抽脂手術
have[get, undergo] liposuction

度過放縱日
have a cheat day

出現溜溜球效應
have a yo-yo effect

運動
work out, exercise, get some exercise(s)

規律地 / 持續地運動
work out regularly/steadily
穿發汗衣運動
work out in a sauna suit
做有氧運動
do aerobic exercise(s)

每天量體重
weigh oneself every day

促進新陳代謝
boost metabolism

BMR - Basal Metabolic Rate

提升基礎代謝率
increase the basal metabolic rate

增加肌肉量
increase muscle mass

減少體脂肪
reduce body fat

SENTENCES TO USE

那名男子做了腹部抽脂手術。
The man had abdominal liposuction.

她正在節食，每週有一天放縱日，
在那天可以想吃什麼就吃什麼。
She's on a diet, so she has a cheat day once a week and eats what she wants that day.

即使大量運動，如果沒有進行飲食控制，
你也無法減去體重。
Even if you work out a lot, you won't lose weight without going on a diet.

想減重，你必須做有氧運動。
You have to do aerobic exercise to lose weight.

如果你想減重並且維持下去，
就應該促進新陳代謝，增加肌肉量。
If you want to lose weight and maintain it, you should boost metabolism and increase your muscle mass.

因意外 / 疾病 / 年老而死亡
die in an accident/from an illness/of old age

孤獨地死去
die alone

孤獨死
solitary death, lonely death

死亡、過世
die, pass away

* pass away 是 die 的婉轉用法，可以翻譯成「逝世、過世」。

自殺、自我結束生命
kill oneself,
commit suicide

把遺體安置在太平間
place a dead body in a mortuary

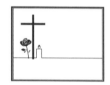

發送～的訃聞
send an obituary of ~

把 B 的死訊告知 A
inform A of B's death

幫遺體淨身穿衣
wash and dress a corpse for burial

SENTENCES TO USE

他的父親去年過世了。
阿爾貝卡繆在46歲時因交通事故去世。
在那國家，2021年有3,159人孤獨地死去。
2020年該國每天約有36人自殺。

His father passed away last year.
Albert Camus died in a car accident at the age of 46.
In that country, 3,159 people died alone in 2021.
In that country in 2020, about 36 people killed themselves a day.

入殮
place the body in the coffin

舉辦喪禮
hold[conduct] a funeral

向哀悼者致意
greet mourners

弔問、表示哀悼
express one's condolences on the death of ~

轉交奠儀
offer condolence money

送弔唁花圈
send
a funeral wreath

SENTENCES TO USE

樞機主教的喪禮在這城市中最大的教堂舉行。
The cardinal's funeral was held in the city's largest cathedral.

往生者的妻子和幼子正在向哀悼者致意。
The deceased's wife and young son were greeting mourners.

我們對她爸爸的過世表示哀悼之意。
We expressed our condolences on the death of her father.

許多政治人物送弔唁花圈到那位新聞記者的父親的喪禮。
Many politicians sent funeral wreaths to the journalist's father's funeral.

出殯
carry a coffin out of the
house[funeral hall]

手持遺像
carry a picture of
the deceased

把棺材抬進靈車
load a coffin into
the hearse

埋葬遺體
bury a body

火葬遺體
cremate a body

手持骨灰罈
carry a burial urn

把骨灰安置在靈骨塔
place somebody's remains
in a charnel house

撒骨灰
scatter someone's ashes

舉行樹葬
bury someone's ashes under a tree,
have someone's ashes buried under a tree

申報～的死亡
report someone's death

SENTENCES TO USE

他拿著已故祖父的遺像走在送葬隊伍的最前面。
He led the funeral procession carrying a picture of his deceased grandfather.

他的遺體火化後，被安置在靈骨塔裡。
His body was cremated and placed in a charnel house.

她要求將她的骨灰撒向大海。
She asked to have her ashes scattered at sea.

近來很多人想要樹葬。
These days many people want to have their ashes buried under a tree.

舉行祭祀
have[hold] an ancestral rite

舉行祭奠、追悼會
hold[have] a memorial service

掃墓、到墓前悼念
visit someone's grave
(and have a memorial service there)

SENTENCES TO USE

越來越多的家庭進行簡單的祭祀。
More and more families hold simple ancestral rites.

今天為事故罹難者舉行追悼會。
Today, a memorial service was held for the victims of the accident.

他前往巴黎到吉姆莫里森的墓前悼念。
He traveled to Paris to visit Jim Morrison's grave.

PART III

社會生活

動作表達

CHAPTER

1

情感表達與人際關係

EMOTIONS &
RELATIONSHIP

049

留下喜悅的淚水
shed tears of joy,
cry happy tears,
weep for joy, cry with joy

對～狂熱、瘋狂
go wild[crazy, mad]
(about ~), get wildly
excited (about ~)

歡呼
cheer,
shout with joy

歡呼鼓掌
cheer and
clap

歡呼迎接
greet ~ with
loud cheers

歡迎
welcome ~,
be delighted to see[meet] ~

熱情款待～、對～給予貴賓禮遇
show[extend, offer] hospitality to ~,
treat ~ like royalty

稱讚
praise, compliment

反應、給予回應
show a reaction

SENTENCES TO USE

第一名通過終點線的運動員留下喜悅的淚水。

當樂團上台時，樂迷們都陷入瘋狂。

在得知那部電影獲得奧斯卡最佳影片獎的消息後，大家都歡呼起來。

他很高興地迎接來訪的朋友。

她對稱讚別人很有一套。

The athlete who crossed the finish line first shed tears of joy.

When the band appeared on the stage, the fans went wild.

Everyone cheered at the news that the film had won the Academy Award for Best Picture.

He welcomed a friend who was visiting him.

She has a knack for praising people.

生氣
get angry[mad, furious], lose one's temper

發脾氣
throw a tantrum, get irritated

耍脾氣
do something mean, act surly

避免和～眼神接觸
not make eye contact with ~, not look someone in the eye, avoid making eye contact with

勃然大怒
fly into a rage, fly off the handle

大吵大鬧
scream like hell

（因絕望、氣憤）
扯頭髮
tear one's hair out

淚流不止
cry one's eyes out
（意指痛哭到把眼睛都哭出來了）

（氣到）跺腳
stomp one's foot (in anger)

用拳頭猛擊桌子
pound[hit] the desk with one's fist

指責
denounce, condemn

責罵
scold, call down

咒罵
swear (at ~), curse (at ~)

（向～）道歉
apologize (to ~)

SENTENCES TO USE

她對於他的不負責任行為感到生氣。 She got angry at his irresponsible behavior.

我因為連續兩天幾乎沒有睡覺而對大家發脾氣。
I slept very little for two days in a row and got irritated with people.

當她沒有敲門就開門時，他勃然大怒了起來。
He flew into a rage when she opened the door without knocking.

在事故中喪失孩子的母親淚流不止。
The mother of the child, who lost his life in the accident, cried her eyes out.

那男子在聽證會上一邊高聲叫喊，一邊用拳頭猛擊桌子。
The man screamed at the hearing as he pounded the desk with his fist.

流涙
shed tears,
weep

關在室內不出門
shut oneself in,
stay indoors

傾聽
listen (to ~),
be all ears

安慰、鼓舞
console, comfort,
cheer ~ up

鼓勵
encourage

體貼
be considerate to ~

奉承、吹捧
flatter

嫉妒
get jealous

看不起、小看
look down on, belittle

藐視
despise, scorn

嘲笑
laugh at, make fun of,
ridicule, mock

擺架子、裝腔作勢
put on airs

SENTENCES TO USE

她因為無精打采而把自己關在家裡兩天。　Feeling lethargic, she shut herself in her room for two days.

對話的基本是傾聽對方。　The basis of conversation is to listen to the other person.

年幼的女兒安慰了她。　A young daughter comforted her.

他總是盡量替他人著想。　He always tries to be considerate to others.

她往往看不起那些
她認為比不上自己的人。　She tends to look down on people
who she thinks are beneath her.

UNIT

2 關係、糾紛

變得親近
get[become] close (to ~),
make friends (with ~),
become intimate (with ~)

相處融洽
get along (well)
(with ~)

（與～）混在一起、
玩在一起
run around (with ~)

（愛情上的）交往
go out (with ~),
date (~)

吵架
have an argument (with ~),
have words (with ~),
argue[quarrel] (with ~)

爭吵、打架
argue[quarrel]
(with ~), fight (with ~)

關係疏遠
grow apart (from ~),
be estranged (from ~)

對～冷漠、
愛搭不理
give the
cold
shoulder
(to ~)

和好
make up (with ~), make peace (with ~),
reconcile (with ~)

請求和解
ask for
reconciliation

挑撥離間 A 和 B 的關係
drive a wedge between A and B,
turn A against B

SENTENCES TO USE

我們在同一家公司工作的時候，
關係變得親近。

他和班上所有同學都相處融洽。

她今天和她的男朋友吵架。

我和她疏遠已一段時間了。

他挑撥離間大衛和他的老闆。

We became close
while working at the same company.

He gets along well with all his classmates.

She had an argument with her boyfriend today.

I've been estranged from her for some time.

He drove a wedge between David and his boss.

CHAPTER 1 EMOTIONS & RELATIONSHIP **149**

迷戀上～
have a crush on ~

眼光高
have high standards

喜歡上～
have feelings for ~

對～有意思
have a thing for ~

和～關係曖昧
have a thing with ~

對～提出約會邀請
ask ~ out (on a date)

與～交往、約會
go out with ~, date ~

故作冷淡、欲擒故縱
play hard to get

（～期間）在一起
be together for ~

與～分手
break up with ~

復合
get back together

SENTENCES TO USE

我迷戀上了經常在公車站遇見的那位男子。

你最近有和誰關係曖昧嗎？
我現在沒有交往的人。
我不玩欲擒故縱的把戲。
那兩人已經在一起兩年了。

I have a crush on the man I often see at the bus stop.
Is there anyone you have a thing with?
I'm not dating anyone right now.
I don't play hard to get.
The two have been together for about two years.

甩掉、拋棄
dump ~, kick ~

對～不忠
cheat on ~

情侶吵架
have a lovers' quarrel

與～訂婚
get engaged to ~

向～求婚
propose to ~

和～結婚
marry ~,
get married to ~

離婚
get divorced, get a divorce

和～離婚
divorce ~

SENTENCES TO USE

她甩了男朋友，奔向其他男人。	She dumped her boyfriend and went to another man.
那位歌手對他的妻子不忠。	The singer cheated on his wife.
他們這對情侶經常吵架。	They often had lovers' quarrels.
我想與好相處的人結婚。	I want to marry a friendly person.
那位跨國公司的 CEO 與結婚27年的妻子離婚了。	The CEO of the global company divorced his wife after 27 years of marriage.

CHAPTER

2

工作與職業

WORKS & JOBS

（搭乘～）通勤
commute (by ~)

上班
go to work,
go to
the office

下班
leave work, get off work,
leave the office,
be gone for the day

打卡上班
clock in, punch in

打卡下班
clock out,
punch out

開會
have a
meeting

指派工作
assign work

報告工作事項
give a report
of the work

做文書工作
do paperwork

做報告
make[write]
a report

提交待批文件
submit documents for
(someone's) approval

撰寫 / 提交專案企劃書
write/submit
a project proposal

發表簡報
give
a presentation

SENTENCES TO USE

我搭地鐵通勤。

I commute by subway.

員工們在輪班的開始和結束時打卡上下班。

The workers clock in and out at the start and end of each shift.

我們小組每天早上開會，我們部門則是每週開一次會。

Our team has a meeting every morning, and our department has a meeting once a week.

我必須寫一份關於市場調查結果的報告。

I have to write a report on the results of the market research.

他發表了針對那項專案企劃的簡報 。

He gave a presentation on the project proposal.

打電話給客戶
call a client

接聽電話
answer the
call[phone],
take the call[phone]

轉接電話（給他人）
transfer a call

連線公司內部網路
access the
company's Intranet

確認電子郵件
check one's
email

寄電子郵件
send
an email

回覆電子郵件
reply to an email

發送／接收傳真
send/receive
a fax

列印
print out

複印
xerox,
photocopy

與客戶見面
meet one's
client

去～出差
go on[take, be on]
a business trip to ~

到國外出差
go on an overseas
business trip

被上司罵、責備
be chewed out
by one's boss

SENTENCES TO USE

今天我多次打電話給客戶。	I called clients many times today.
我接了電話後並轉接給負責人。	I answered the phone and transferred it to the person in charge.
即使在大家都使用網路的今日，人們偶爾還是會發送傳真。	Even today, when everyone just uses the Internet, there are still times people send faxes.
我這週要去釜山出差。	I'm going on a business trip to Busan this week.
他被上司責備了，所以心情不好。	He is not happy as he was chewed out by his boss.

請假、休假
take a day off[time off, a PTO(personal time off)]
請病假
take sick leave, take a sick day
休年假
take annual[yearly] leave, go on annual leave

放暑假
go on[take] a summer holiday[vacation]

加班
work overtime

領加班費
get overtime pay, get paid overtime

在假日工作
work on a holiday

上班遲到
be late for work

提交道歉信（與事情經過說明）
submit a written apology (and explanation)

SENTENCES TO USE

我今天預約醫院看診，所以請一天假。
I took a PTO today for a doctor's appointment.

他今天早上感覺自己好像感冒了，所以請一天病假。
He felt like he had a cold this morning, so he took a sick day.

最近我只要加班，就能領加班費。
These days, if I work overtime, I get overtime pay.

年輕時，我不只是加班，也在假日工作。
When I was young, I worked not only overtime but also on holidays.

他為了那次事件寫了一份道歉信。
He submitted a written apology for the incident.

（與同事）聚餐
get together (with coworkers)
for dinner or drinks

協商年薪
negotiate for one's annual salary

領薪水
get[draw] a salary, get paid

加薪
get a pay raise

減薪
get a pay cut

SENTENCES TO USE

昨天組員們晚上聚餐歡迎新員工。
The team members got together for dinner yesterday to welcome the new employee.

我針對年薪進行談判，並獲得小幅度的加薪。
I negotiated for my annual salary and I got a small pay raise.

我在每個月25日領薪水。
I get paid on the 25th of every month.

領取獎金
get[receive] a bonus

預支
get an advance,
get[draw, receive] 金額
in advance

取得在職證明書
get a copy of one's
certificate[proof]
of employment

招聘新員工
recruit new
employees[workers]

聘請新員工
hire[engage] new
employees[workers]

訓練新員工
train new
employees[workers]

經過試用期
have[go through]
a probation period

開發專業（工作）技能
do professional
development

遞交辭呈
hand in one's
notice[resignation]

SENTENCES TO USE

今年公司創下銷售佳績，
因此我們得到豐厚的年終獎金。

The company's sales were good this year, so we received a generous year-end bonus.

申請簽證時，你必須取得在職證明書。

To apply for a visa, you must get a copy of your certificate of employment.

那間公司正在招聘新員工。

The company is recruiting new employees.

新員工有三個月的試用期。

New employees have a three-month probation period.

向繼任者交接／説明業務（職責）
hand over/explain one's duties
[responsibilities] to one's successor

辭職
resign
(from a company)

被升職
be[get] promoted,
get a promotion

晉升為～
be[get]
promoted (to ~)

換工作
change one's job,
move to another company

被解雇
get[be] fired, get[be] laid off

退休、解職
retire (from ~)

SENTENCES TO USE

在離開公司前，你必須向
繼任者説明你的職責。

You need to explain your responsibilities to your successor before leaving the company.

上個月她被晉升為組長。

She was promoted to team leader last month.

我明年會跳槽到另一間公司。

I will move to another company next year.

從教職退休後，他開始畫畫。

After retiring from teaching, he began drawing.

開店、開始營業
open the store

打烊、停止營業
close the store

接待顧客
greet[meet]
customers

回應顧客的詢問
respond to
customer inquiries

接單、點菜
take an order

（店員）結帳
ring up

包裝（商品）
wrap ~

滿足顧客需求
meet the needs
of customers

呼叫號碼 / 名字
call the
number/name

處理錯誤的訂單
handle[deal with]
wrong orders

累積點數
earn[collect] (reward/
bonus) points

回應顧客的抱怨
respond to customer
complaints

SENTENCES TO USE

他們早上10點開店。

那位員工總是面帶笑容地接待顧客。

當我回應顧客的詢問時，一天很快就過去了。

我在那家超市買東西時，總是可以累積點數。

They open the store at 10 a.m.

The employee always greets customers with a smile.

The day flies by when I'm responding to customer inquiries.

I always earn reward points when I buy things at the supermarket.

接聽電話
answer[get] a call

打電話到客服中心
call a customer service center

聽取詢問事項
listen to inquiries

提供諮詢（資訊或建議）
provide information
or advice

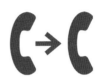

轉接電話給負責單位
transfer a call to the
department in charge

錄下通話內容
record phone conversations

採取必要的後續措施
follow up on the necessary measures,
take necessary follow-up measures

SENTENCES TO USE

據説客服中心人員一天要接大約80通電話。
The call center agent is said to get about 80 calls a day.

接聽電話時，你應該仔細傾聽顧客的詢問。
When you answer a call, you should listen to the customer's inquiries carefully.

他把電話轉接給負責單位。
He transferred the call to the department in charge.

她與客戶通話後，採取了必要的後續措施。
She talked to the customer and followed up on the necessary measures.

搭乘公車上下班
take a commuter bus to and from work,
go to and from work by commuter bus

感應員工識別證
scan employee
ID card

進行保安 / 安全檢查
conduct a security/
safety check

換上工作服
change into one's work
clothes[workwear]

穿防塵服 / 穿防塵鞋 / 戴手套 / 戴口罩
wear dustproof clothes/
dustproof shoes/gloves/masks

（在空氣浴塵室）除塵
take an air shower

檢查機器
check[inspect]
a machine

驗收產品
inspect products

找出不良品
pick out defective
products

兩班 / 三班制工作
work in two/three
shifts

SENTENCES TO USE

他搭乘公車上下班。

他們進入大樓時要感應員工識別證。

他們值勤時必須穿戴手套和口罩。

在半導體工廠，他們在進入無塵室前必須先在空氣浴塵室除塵。

他們工作是輪三班制。

He takes a commuter bus to and from work.

They scan their employee ID card when they enter the building.

They have to wear gloves and masks while on duty.

In a semiconductor factory, they have to take an air shower before entering a clean room.

They work in three shifts.

加班、超時工作
work overtime,
work extra hours

休息一下
have a break

在員工餐廳吃午餐
have[eat] lunch
in the cafeteria

住工廠員工宿舍
live in a factory
dormitory

移交業務給～
hand over one's
duties[responsibilities] to ~

引導視察團隊
guide the field
inspection team

遭遇職災、工安意外
be[get] injured in a workplace
accident, have an accident at work,
have a workplace accident

組成工會
form a labor
union

勞資協商破裂
the talks between
labor and management
broke down

罷工
go on
strike

SENTENCES TO USE

由於訂單數量龐大，這個月大家
都加了很多班。

通常我在員工餐廳吃早餐和午餐。

她住在工廠員工宿舍。

他在一次工安意外中受傷。

勞資雙方的協議破裂，
勞工們開始罷工。

Everyone worked overtime a lot this month because
of the high volume of orders.

Usually I have breakfast and lunch in the cafeteria.

She lives in a factory dormitory.

The man was injured in a workplace accident.

The talks between labor and management broke
down and the workers went on strike.

農業

種植稻米 / 大白菜 / 豆子等
farm rice/Chinese cabbage/beans …

用耕耘機 / 牽引機翻土
work the land with a cultivator/tractor

灌溉稻田
irrigate a rice paddy

準備苗床
prepare seedbeds

插秧
plant rice, plant young rice plants

使用水稻插秧機
use a rice planting machine

施肥
fertilize

空中噴藥（飛機、無人機噴灑農藥）
crop-dust

收割、收獲稻米
harvest rice

排出稻田的水
drain a rice paddy

用烘乾機烘乾稻穀
dry rice with a rice dryer

在碾米廠脫稻穀的殼
dehusk rice at a rice mill

SENTENCES TO USE

他們開始務農並種植草莓。
They took up farming and farm strawberries.

現在人們使用水稻插秧機插秧。
These days, people plant rice using rice planting machines.

他們使用牽引機幫稻田施肥。
They are fertilizing rice fields with a tractor.

他們通常從九月底到十月初收割稻子。
They usually harvest rice from late September to early October.

你在烹煮稻米前必須先去殼。
You have to dehusk rice before you can cook it.

播種
sow seeds

種植幼苗
plant a seedling

除草、拔草
weed out, pull out
weeds, root out weeds

在田裡施肥
spread manure on a field

噴灑農藥
spray[dust] (agricultural) pesticide

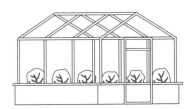

在溫室栽培～
grow ~ in greenhouses

收成
harvest ~

SENTENCES TO USE

我媽媽今年又在她的菜園裡種植辣椒苗。

你必須拔掉田裡的雜草。

這個萵苣在種植時沒有噴灑農藥。

他們在溫室裡栽種橘子。

My mom planted pepper seedlings in her kitchen garden again this year.

You have to pull out the weeds in the field.

This lettuce is grown without spraying pesticides.

They grow tangerines in greenhouses.

水產業

出海捕魚
go out to the sea,
go fishing

從事養殖、經營養魚場
run a fish farm,
raise fish in a fish farm

撒網
cast a net
收網
draw[haul] in a net

拋錨使漁船停泊
anchor
a fishing boat

捕魚作業結束後返回
return from
fishing

分配 / 儲藏捕獲的海產
divide/store the catch

在漁市場拍賣漁獲
auction the catch
at the fish market

修理漁具
repair[mend]
fishing gear

SENTENCES TO USE

漁夫們在太陽升起前早早出海去捕魚。
The fishermen go fishing early in the morning before the sun rises.
他們在海上的養魚場養殖比目魚。
They raise flatfish in a fish farm in the sea.
我看過漁夫們在漁市場拍賣漁獲。
I have seen fishermen auction the catch at the fish market.
漁夫們結束捕魚作業，正在修理他們的漁具。
The fishermen have finished fishing and are repairing their fishing gear.

生產
produce

流通、配送
distribute

消費
consume

銷售
sell

購買
buy, purchase

經商、做買賣
do business

與～做生意
do business
with ～

投資在～
invest in ～

打工兼職
work part-time

把錢存入銀行
deposit money
in a bank

賺取利息
earn interest

取得貸款
get a loan

投資股票
invest in stocks

領取股息
receive
a dividend

SENTENCES TO USE

那家公司使用國產米製作馬格利酒。 The company produces makgeolli made from domestic rice.

那個國家消費大量的蒜頭。 The country consumes a lot of garlic.

她從大學一年級開始兼差到現在。 She has worked part-time since she was a freshman in college.

貸款越來越難了。 It's getting harder and harder to get a loan.

最近有很多20多歲的人投資股票。 Many people in their 20s invest in stocks these days.

3

購物

SHOPPING

實體商店購物 ① -
便利商店、超市、傳統市場、大型量販店

 057

挑選商品
choose goods

比較商品 / 價格
compare goods/
prices

詢問～的價格
ask the price of ~

詢問商品
ask about
goods[products]

把～放入購物車
put ~ in the cart

把～放入購物袋
put ~ in the
shopping bag

結帳
pay for ~

討價還價、殺價
（商人 / 消費者）
haggle over the price
（消費者）
ask for a lower price

獲得～免費贈品
get ~ as a free gift
附贈～
throw ~ in
（商人）給優惠價
give someone a deal

SENTENCES TO USE

我比較價格後購買商品。

在大型商場很難找到可以詢問商品的員工。

他從貨架上選取商品並放入購物車。

有些人會在傳統市場對商品討價還價。

I buy products after comparing prices.

It is difficult to find employees to ask about products in large stores.

He picked things off the shelves and put them in the cart.

There are people who haggle over the prices of goods at the traditional market.

累積點數
earn[collect]
(reward/bonus) points

使用會員卡享有優惠
get a discount with
a partner membership card

使用斜坡輸送帶
use a moving walkway
[moving sidewalk]

將購買的物品放入後車廂
put[load] the purchased goods
[items] in the trunk of a car

宅配購買的物品
have the purchased
goods[items] delivered

SENTENCES TO USE

她每次購物都不忘累積點數。
She doesn't forget to earn reward points every time she buys something.
在那家便利商店憑會員卡可以享有優惠。
You can get a discount at that convenience store with a partner membership card.
在我把購買的商品放進後車廂時，電話響了。
The phone rang when I was loading the purchased items in the trunk of the car.
我讓人把我在超市購買的商品宅配到我家。
I had the goods I had bought at the supermarket delivered to my house.

挑選商品
choose goods

詢問尺寸
ask about the size (of ~)

試穿（衣服）、試戴
（飾品配件等）
try on ~, try ~ on

確認價格
check the price (of ~)

詢問價格
ask about the price (of ~)

結帳
pay for ~

設定配送日期
set a delivery date

只逛不買、櫥窗購物
go window-shopping

在免稅店購買～
buy[purchase]
~ at a duty-free shop

以免稅價格購買～
buy[purchase] ~
duty free

出示護照和登機證
present one's
passport and
boarding pass

在機場提貨櫃檯領取物品
collect the items at the
pick-up desk[counter]
at the airport

SENTENCES TO USE

我向店員詢問洋裝的尺寸。
I asked the staff about the size of the dress.

在購買褲子前你應該先試穿看看。
You should try on pants before buying them.

她以免稅價格買了一個外國品牌的包包。
She bought a bag from a foreign brand duty free.

我們必須在免稅店出示護照和登機證。
We must present our passports and boarding passes at a duty-free shop.

我在機場提貨櫃檯領取我在市區
免稅店購買的物品。
I collected my purchase from the duty-free shop in the city at the airport pick-up counter.

美容美髮服務

美髮店、按摩院　　　　　　　　　　　　* 本頁美髮相關表達皆為髮型設計師工作時的用語。

做頭髮
have[get]
one's
hair done

剪頭髮
have[get] one's
hair cut, have
[get] a haircut

把頭髮剪短
have[get]
one's hair
cut short

剪平頭
get a buzz cut

把頭髮剃光
have[get] one's
hair shaved
completely

修剪頭髮
have[get] one's
hair trimmed

燙頭髮
have[get] one's hair permed,
have[get] a perm

染頭髮
have[get] one's
hair dyed

洗頭髮
have[get] one's
hair washed

吹乾頭髮
have[get] one's hair
blow-dried

在做頭髮時看雜誌
read a magazine while
having one's hair done

被化妝
have[get] one's
makeup done

被按摩
get a massage

SENTENCES TO USE

他每個月剪頭髮。	He gets a haircut every month.
我隔了很久才剪頭髮和燙頭髮。	I had my hair cut and got my hair permed after a long time.
他在入伍時剪了平頭。	He got a buzz cut when he entered the army.
我因為白頭髮的緣故， 必須每個月去染一次頭髮。	I have to have my hair dyed once a month because of my gray hair.
她把頭髮染成藍色。	She had her hair dyed blue.

美甲店

做指甲
have[get] one's nails done, have[get] a manicure

挑選指甲造型
choose nail designs

做光療指甲
have gel nails
applied

在手指甲上做光療指甲
apply gel nails
on (finger)nails

卸除光療指甲
have gel nails
removed

（自己）卸除光療指甲
remove[take off]
gel nails

在指甲上貼美甲貼
put nail stickers
on (finger)nails

卸除美甲貼
remove nail
stickers

做腳趾甲
have[get] one's
toenails done

做手指甲 / 腳趾甲護理
have one's fingernails/
toenails cared

做足部去角質
get the dead
skin removed
from one's feet

SENTENCES TO USE

她偶爾會在美甲店做指甲。	She sometimes gets her nails done at the nail salon.
現今人們做光療指甲是常有的事。	Nowadays, people often have gel nails applied.
很多人不去美甲店，而是在家貼美甲貼在指甲上。	Many people put nail stickers on their nails at home instead of going to the nail salon.
我在夏天會做腳趾甲。	I have my toenails done in summer.
她在美甲店做足部去角質。	She got the dead skin removed from her feet at the nail salon.

網路購物
shop
online

在～訂購～
order ~
at[from] …

選擇～（產品）
choose ~

比較商品／價格
compare
goods/prices

把～加入購物車
add ~ to one's[the]
(shopping) cart

使用折扣券
apply a discount
coupon

支付運費
pay for delivery,
pay for shipping

輸入收件地址
enter the shipping
address

輸入個人清關認
證碼
enter one's
PCCC (personal
customs
clearance code)

結帳
make a payment

使用點數（紅利點數）
use (bonus/reward) points

把～加入願望清單
add ~ to
one's wishlist

SENTENCES TO USE

我在網路書店訂購他的新書。
I ordered his new book from an online bookstore.

網路購物能夠讓你輕鬆比價。
You can easily compare prices when shopping online.

若消費金額在5萬韓元以下，
就必須支付運費。
If the purchase price is less than 50,000 won,
you have to pay for delivery.

直購海外商品時，
必須輸入你的個人清關認證碼。
When you buy overseas goods directly, you must
enter your personal customs clearance code.

查看訂單詳細內容
check the details of
an order

查看配送狀態
check the tracking
information

向賣家提問
leave[post] a question
to the seller

向賣家投訴交貨延誤
complain to the seller
about delayed delivery

把 A 換成 B
exchange A for B

退貨
return ~

取得退款
get a refund

撰寫心得
write a review

上傳心得與照片
post a review
with a photo

SENTENCES TO USE

他查詢了兩天前訂購的運動鞋配送狀態。 He checked the tracking information for the sneakers he had ordered two days earlier.

我向賣家提問了關於交貨日期的問題。 I posted a question to the seller regarding the delivery date.

她把一個粉紅色的靠墊換成灰色的。 She exchanged a pink cushion for a gray one.

我在網路上購買的鞋子太小，
所以我把它們退貨了。 The shoes I bought online were too small, so I returned them.

她上傳了一篇關於
她網購洋裝的心得和照片。 She posted a review of the dress she had bought online along with a photo.

There are people who
haggle over the prices of goods
at the traditional market.

CHAPTER

4

生產與育兒

CHILDBIRTH & PARENTING

懷孕、生產

驗孕
take a
pregnancy test

在醫院確認懷孕
confirm one's
pregnancy
at a hospital

懷孕
be pregnant (with ~),
have a baby

懷有雙胞胎 / 三胞胎
be pregnant with
twins/triplets

8 months
懷孕～週 / 月
be ~ weeks/
months
pregnant

撰寫媽媽手冊
write in the new mother's
notebook[diary],
write in the pregnancy diary

服用葉酸 / 鐵劑
take folic acid/
iron pills

做超音波檢查
get[take, have]
an ultrasound

做畸形兒篩檢
get[take, have]
an abnormality
screening test

做胎兒染色體檢查
get[take, have] a fetal
chromosome test

罹患妊娠糖尿病
suffer from
gestational diabetes

罹患妊娠高血壓
suffer from gestational
hypertension

孕吐
have morning
sickness

SENTENCES TO USE

我在家裡做了驗孕，
之後在醫院確定我懷孕了。

I took a pregnancy test at home and then confirmed my pregnancy at the hospital.

我的姐姐懷了雙胞胎。

My sister is pregnant with twins.

她懷孕27週了。

She is 27 weeks pregnant.

你也必須在懷孕初期做胎兒染色體檢查。

You also need to get a fetal chromosome test early in the pregnancy.

我幾乎沒有孕吐。

I hardly ever had morning sickness.

為了胎教而做～
do ~ for prenatal
education

購買新生兒用品
buy newborn baby
products

佈置嬰兒房
decorate
a nursery

待產中
be expecting a baby,
be due (to give birth)

出現陣痛
have labor pains,
have contractions

每隔～分鐘陣痛一次
have contractions
[labor pains]
every ~ minutes
[~ minutes apart]

羊水破了
one's water broke

分娩中、陣痛中
be in labor

自然產生下～
give birth to ~ naturally,
have ~ by natural
childbirth

剖腹產生下～
deliver ~
by Caesarean
section

剪臍帶
cut the umbilical
cord

生下～
give birth to ~

將孩子從產房移到新生兒室
move a baby from
the delivery room
to the neonatal unit

SENTENCES TO USE

她在生產前購買了新生兒用品，
也佈置了嬰兒房。

She bought newborn baby products and decorated
the nursery before giving birth.

我女兒預計下週出生。

My daughter is due next week.

她正在陣痛中。

She's in labor.

那位產婦每隔10分鐘陣痛一次。

The mother has contractions every 10 minutes.

她今天生下一名女嬰。

She gave birth to a baby girl today.

獲得政府生育獎勵金
get government benefits
for having a baby

難產
have a hard labor

早產
give birth prematurely,
have the baby arrive early

死產、胎死腹中
have a stillbirth,
give birth to a stillborn
(baby)

流產
miscarry

無法生育
cannot have a baby, cannot get pregnant,
be unable to conceive

女方 / 男方不孕
the woman/the man
is infertile

看不孕症門診
go to a fertility clinic

確認排卵日
check one's
ovulation day

SENTENCES TO USE

那名女子在懷孕8個月時早產。
The woman gave birth prematurely when she was eight months pregnant.

在生下第一個女兒以前，她曾經流產過一次。
She miscarried once before giving birth to her first daughter.

那對夫妻因為無法生育而長期飽受煎熬。
The couple suffered for a long time because they couldn't have a baby.

嘗試自然懷孕
try to conceive
[get pregnant] naturally

做人工授精
do artificial
insemination

做試管嬰兒（體外授精）
do IVF(in vitro fertilization)

冷凍卵子
freeze one's eggs

使用精子銀行的精子
use sperm from a sperm bank

透過代理孕母生小孩
give birth to a baby
through a surrogate mother

SENTENCES TO USE

在嘗試幾次人工授精後，我們透過試管嬰兒生下了孩子。
We tried artificial insemination a few times before giving birth to a baby through in vitro fertilization.
越來越多的女性在年輕時冷凍他們的卵子。
More and more women freeze their eggs when they are young.
那位女性使用精子銀行的精子生下一名兒子。
The woman gave birth to a son with sperm from a sperm bank.

2 育兒

餵母乳
breastfeed
one's baby

用奶瓶餵奶
bottle-feed
one's baby

使嬰兒打嗝
burp
one's baby

抱小孩
hold
one's baby

把嬰兒背在背上
carry one's baby
on one's back

讓嬰兒乘坐嬰兒車
take one's baby in a stroller
[baby carriage,
pram, pushchair]

幫嬰兒洗澡
give one's baby
a bath,
bathe one's baby

安撫哭啼的嬰兒
soothe[calm]
a crying baby

安撫折騰人的 / 哭鬧的
嬰兒
soothe one's upset/
whining baby

更換尿布
change
the diaper

把嬰兒放在床上
lay one's baby
on the bed

設法讓嬰兒睡著
put one's baby
to sleep

哄嬰兒入睡
lull one's baby
to sleep

唱搖籃曲給嬰兒聽
sing a lullaby
to one's baby

SENTENCES TO USE

可能的話，我想用母乳餵食我的孩子。
在餵完母乳後，你必須使嬰兒打嗝。
那男子把嬰兒背在背上。
很難安撫一個哭鬧的嬰兒。
那對夫妻輪流哄嬰兒睡覺。

I want to breastfeed my child if possible.
You should burp your baby after breastfeeding them.
The man carried the baby on his back.
It's hard to soothe a crying baby.
The couple take turns putting their baby to sleep.

完全獨自撫養小孩
raise one's child
entirely alone

把孩子託付給～
leave one's baby
with ~

請產假（陪產假）
take maternity
[paternity] leave

休產假（陪產假）中
be on maternity
[paternity] leave

與～眼神接觸
make eye contact
(with ~)

製作副食品
make baby food
[baby weaning food]

幫嬰兒戴圍兜
put a bib
on one's baby

使嬰兒乘坐學步車
put one's baby
in a baby walker

訓練嬰兒走路
teach one's baby to walk,
help a baby learn to walk

訓練嬰兒如廁
toilet train one's child,
potty-train one's child

訓練嬰兒使用湯匙 / 筷子
teach one's baby to use
a spoon/chopsticks

SENTENCES TO USE

她白天把孩子託付給媽媽後再去上班。

現在越來越多男性請陪產假。

出生4週後，嬰兒開始會與人眼神接觸。

她最近很喜歡做嬰兒副食品。

我最近在訓練我的孩子上廁所。

She leaves her baby with her mother during the day and goes to work.

These days, more and more men are taking paternity leave.

At four weeks of age, the baby begins to make eye contact.

She is into making baby food these days.

I'm toilet training my child these days.

慶祝～的出生百日
celebrate one's 100th day

舉辦周歲派對
have[throw] a first birthday party

申請 / 領取育兒津貼
apply for/get the childcare allowance[child benefit]

讓孩子接種疫苗
get one's child vaccinated

帶孩子做健康檢查
take the child to the pediatrician for a (regular) check-up

（孩子）耍脾氣
have[throw] a tantrum

唸書給～聽
read ~ a book, read to ~

給～看智慧型手機 / YouTube 影片 / 電視
show ~ smartphone/ YouTube videos/TV

送～上托育中心 / 幼稚園 / 小學
send ~ to daycare center/ kindergarten/elementary school

與孩子的老師商談
consult one's child's teacher

輔導學習～的課業
help ~ study 科目, help ~ with 科目 studies

SENTENCES TO USE

我們夫妻在上週六慶祝孩子出生100天。
明天我要帶孩子去接種疫苗。
他每天晚上在孩子睡覺前
都會唸書給孩子聽。

很多父母為了讓孩子保持安靜而讓
他們看智慧型手機上的 YouTube 影片。

她每天下班後都輔導她的女兒學習
英文和數學。

My wife and I celebrated our child's 100th day last Saturday.
I'm going to get my child vaccinated tomorrow.
He reads to his child every night before he goes to bed.

Many parents show their children YouTube videos on their smartphones when they want to keep them quiet.

She helps her daughter study English and math after work every day.

派～跑腿辦事
send ~ on an errand (to 動詞原型),
make ~ run an errand (to 動詞原型)

叫～做家事
have[make] ~ do
housework[chores]

幫～建立好習慣
help ~ build[develop]
a good habit

讓～累積各種經驗
have ~ experience many things

稱讚
praise ~

鼓勵
encourage ~

斥責
scold ~

與～講道理、勸服
reason with ~,
persuade ~

生～的氣
get angry with ~,
get mad at ~

控制～
control ~

SENTENCES TO USE

她叫她的小孩幫忙跑腿買些醬油。
不讓你的小孩做任何家事是件好事嗎？
想要讓孩子養成好習慣，
父母必須有好習慣。
我們試著讓孩子累積許多經驗。
我認為經常稱讚和鼓勵孩子是件好事。

She sent her child on an errand to buy some soy sauce.
Is it good not to have your child do any housework?
Parents must have good habits to help their children develop good habits.
We try to have our child experience many things.
I think it's good to praise and encourage children often.

送～上家教課
send ~ to
a (private) lesson

送～上補習班
send ~ to
a private academy

送～去上英文 / 數學 / 鋼琴 / 美術課
send ~ to an English/a math/
a piano/an art lesson

（聘請老師）上～家教課
have a ~ tutor

幫助～找到個人性向
help ~ find one's aptitude

讓～接受適時教育
give ~ timely education

SENTENCES TO USE

韓國父母送他們的孩子去上很多家教課。
Korean parents send their children to many private lessons.

她讓她的小孩上英文課、數學課和鋼琴課。
She sends her child to English, math, and piano lessons.

父母應該幫助孩子找到他們的性向。
Parents should help their children find their aptitude.

孩子們需要的不是早期教育，而是適時教育。
What children need is not early education, but timely education.

送～去校外教學
send ~ on a field trip

參加父母教學觀摩
attend an open class
for parents

讓～轉學到其他學校
transfer ~ to
another school

送～去（早期）留學
send ~ to study
abroad (at an early age)

送～上變通學校
send ~ to an
alternative school

* 一種組織和教育內容
較彈性的學校

讓～做智力測驗
have ~ get an IQ test

閱讀育兒書籍
read books on parenting

SENTENCES TO USE

我去我女兒學校參加父母教學觀摩。
I attended an open class for parents at my daughter's school.
他在兒子讀國中時送他出國留學。
He sent his son to study abroad when he was in middle school.
那對父母把在校表現不佳的兒子送去上變通學校。
The parents sent their child who had not done well at school to an alternative school.
她對教育很感興趣，因此喜歡閱讀育兒書籍。
She likes reading books on parenting as she's interested in education.

CHAPTER

5

休閒與興趣

LEISURE & HOBBIES

旅行

去（～地點）旅行
travel (to ~), take a trip (to ~),
go on a trip (to ~),
go on a journey (to ~)

打包行李
pack for one's journey,
pack one's bag
[suitcase, luggage]

去（～地點）一日遊
take a day trip (to ~),
go on a day trip (to ~)

去～天～夜旅行
travel for ~ nights and
… days

國內旅行
travel within one's
home country

出國旅行
travel abroad

背包旅行
go backpacking,
go on a backpacking trip

套裝行程旅遊
go on a package
tour

搭乘遊輪旅行
go on a cruise

SENTENCES TO USE

疫情結束後，我想去美國旅行。　　When the pandemic is over, I want to travel to the United States.

我們家常去鄉下一日遊。　　My family often goes on a day trip to the country.

幾年前我去義大利旅行，
在那裡停留了八天七夜。　　A few years ago, I traveled to Italy and stayed for 7 nights and 8 days.

她在20幾歲時去背包旅行50天。　　She went backpacking for 50 days when she was in her 20s.

去校外教學
go on
a school trip

graduation trip

去畢業旅行
go on
a graduation trip

去蜜月旅行
go on
a honeymoon

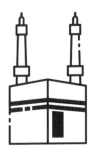

前往橫跨全國之旅
go on a cross-country trip

MAP

前往實地考察
go on a field trip to explore ~

去～朝聖
go on[make]
a pilgrimage to ~

環遊世界
travel around
the world

SENTENCES TO USE

他們去濟州島畢業旅行。 　 They went on a graduation trip to Jeju Island.

她在大學時期橫跨全國旅行。 　 She went on a cross-country trip when she was in college.

他們去梵蒂岡朝聖。 　 They went on a pilgrimage to the Vatican.

他中了彩券，決定去環遊世界。 　 He won the lottery and decided to travel around the world.

擬定旅行計畫
plan a trip,
make a tour plan

規劃旅行路線
set a route
for a trip

預訂飯店房間 / 旅館 / 民宿 / 愛彼迎
book[reserve] a hotel room/
a hostel/a B&B/an Airbnb

預訂（前往～的）
火車票 / 公車票 / 機票
book a train ticket/a bus ticket/
a plane ticket[a flight] (to ~)

購買（前往～的）火
車票 / 公車票 / 機票
buy a train ticket/
a bus ticket/
a plane ticket
[a flight] (to ~)

搭乘汽車 / 火車 /
公車 / 飛機前往
go by car/train/
bus/plane

搭乘飛機 / 火車 / 公車（去～）旅行
travel (to) ~
by plane/train/bus

換乘飛機 / 火車 / 公車
change planes/
trains/buses

SENTENCES TO USE

有時候制定旅行計畫比旅行更令人興奮。
Sometimes planning a trip is more exciting than traveling.

他預訂了暑假前往巴黎的機票。
He booked a flight to Paris for his summer vacation.

我們開車去舊金山。
We went to San Francisco by car.

在前往哥本哈根的途中，他們在倫敦轉機。
They changed planes in London on their way to Copenhagen.

住飯店 / 旅館 / 民宿 / 愛彼迎
stay at a hotel/a hostel/
a B&B/an Airbnb

在～辦理入住
check in at ~

在～辦理退房
check out of ~

使用飯店自助餐服務 / 在飯店自助餐用餐
use a hotel buffet/
eat at a hotel buffet

在旅遊服務中心詢問旅遊資訊
ask about travel information at
a tourist information center

租車
rent a car

短暫停留在高速公路休息站
stop by[at] a highway
service[rest] area

在高速公路休息站用餐
have a meal at a highway
service[rest] area

SENTENCES TO USE

我住在英國威爾斯的一家民宿。

他們在火車站附近的一家飯店辦理入住。

她在火車站裡的旅遊服務中心詢問一些
旅遊資訊。

在去目的地的路上，我們在高速公路
休息站吃了簡餐。

I stayed at a B&B in Wales, in the UK.

They checked in at a hotel near the train station.

She asked about some travel information at the tourist
information center at the train station.

We had a light meal at the highway service area on the way
to the destination.

去旅遊景點
go to[visit]
a tourist attraction

參加導覽行程
take part in
[participate in]
a guided tour

享受購物 / 觀光
enjoy shopping/
sightseeing

去美食餐廳
go to a good[famous]
restaurant

尋找美食餐廳
look for a
good[famous]
restaurant

查看美食餐廳的評論
look at the reviews
of good[famous]
restaurants

拍～的照片
take pictures of ~

請～幫忙拍～的照片
ask ~ to take a picture of …

買紀念品
buy a souvenir

SENTENCES TO USE

我參加了羅浮宮的導覽行程。　　　　　　I participated in a guided tour at the Louvre Museum.

中國遊客喜歡在那個都市裡購物、觀光。

The Chinese tourists enjoyed shopping and sightseeing in the city.

有些人旅行時總是會去著名的美食餐廳。

Some people always go to famous restaurants when they go on a trip.

他獨自旅行，所以請其他遊客幫他拍照。

He was traveling alone, so he asked another traveler to take a picture of him.

當我去旅行時，我會買一個小紀念品，用來記住那個地方。

When I go on a trip, I buy a small souvenir to remember that place.

在機場免稅店購買～
buy ~
at the airport duty-free shop

接受安全檢查
get a security check

通過安全檢查
pass through security

通過入境檢查站
pass through the
immigration checkpoint

在行李提取處領取行李
pick up one's luggage
at the baggage claim area

通過海關
go[pass] through
customs

結束旅行回來
return[come back]
from one's trip
[travel, journey]

在社群媒體／部落格發布旅遊照片和心得
post photos[pictures] and reviews
of one's trip on one's SNS/blog

SENTENCES TO USE

在我旅行回程的路上，我在機場免稅店買了一些零食。
On my way back from my trip, I bought some snacks at the airport duty-free shop.

通過安全檢查時，你必須脫下帽子和鞋子。
You have to take off your hat and shoes to pass through security.

通過入境檢查站後，我在行李提取處領取我的行李。
After passing through the immigration checkpoint, I picked up my luggage at the baggage claim area.

旅行回來後，我會在部落格上發布照片和心得感想。
After I come back from a trip, I post pictures and reviews on my blog.

電視、YouTube、Netflix

看電視
watch TV

用 VOD（隨選視訊）看電視節目
watch TV shows through
VOD services

用遙控器切換電視頻道
change the TV channel
by a remote (control)

在 IPTV（網路協定
電視）上看電影
watch a movie
on IPTV

快速瀏覽各個電視頻道
quickly scan through
different TV channels

觀看 YouTube 影片
watch a YouTube video,
watch a video on YouTube

訂閱YouTube 頻道
subscribe to
a YouTube channel

觀看 YouTube 直播
watch a YouTube
live stream

對 YouTube
影片按「讚」
like a video on
YouTube

COMMENT

於 YouTube 影片留言
post a comment on
a YouTube video

下載YouTube影片／音樂
download videos/
music from YouTube

SENTENCES TO USE

現今你可以透過 VOD 觀看過去的電視節目。

Nowadays, you can watch old TV shows through VOD services.

不用去電影院，透過 IPTV 你就可以在家觀看最新電影。

You can watch the latest movies on IPTV at home without going to the theater.

他每天花三個小時以上看 YouTube 影片。

He watches YouTube videos for more than three hours every day.

我訂閱了一位影評人的 YouTube 頻道。

I subscribe to a movie critic's YouTube channel.

有些人會在 YouTube 影片下發表無禮的評論。

There are people who post rude comments on YouTube videos.

開設 YouTube 頻道
open a
YouTube channel

在 YouTube 上直播
live stream
on YouTube

拍攝 / 製作影片
上傳到 YouTube
shoot/make a video to
upload to[on] YouTube

編輯要上傳到
YouTube 的影片
edit a video to upload
to[on] YouTube

上傳影片到
YouTube
upload a video
to[on] YouTube

訂閱 Netflix
subscribe to Netflix

觀看 Netflix
watch Netflix

在 Netflix 觀看電視節目 / 電影 / 紀錄片
watch a TV show/
a movie/a documentary on Netflix

取消訂閱 Netflix
cancel one's Netflix subscription

SENTENCES TO USE

編輯一支要上傳到 YouTube 的
20分鐘影片，大約需要8個小時。

It takes about eight hours to edit a 20-minute video to upload to YouTube.

這位 YouTuber 一週上傳兩支影片
到他的 YouTube 頻道。

The YouTuber uploads two videos a week on his YouTube channel.

我在上週訂閱了 Netflix。

I subscribed to Netflix last week.

他的興趣是看 Netflix 上的紀錄片。

Her hobby is watching documentaries on Netflix.

我雖然訂閱了 Netflix，但幾乎沒看，
於是我在幾個月後就取消訂閱了。

I subscribed to Netflix, but I barely watched it, so I canceled my subscription after a few months.

去看足球／棒球／籃球／排球比賽
go to see a soccer/baseball/
basketball/volleyball game

看足球／棒球／籃球／排球比賽
watch a soccer/baseball/
basketball/volleyball game

踢足球／打棒球／打籃球／打排球
play soccer/baseball/
basketball/volleyball

打羽毛球／網球／桌球／高爾夫球
play badminton/tennis/
table tennis[ping pong]/golf

去慢跑／游泳／爬山／健行／滑雪／溜冰
go jogging/swimming/mountain climbing/
hiking/skiing/skating

跑馬拉松
run a marathon

享受極限運動，例如高空彈
跳和高空跳傘
enjoy extreme sports
such as bunjee jumping
and sky diving

SENTENCES TO USE

我上小學的時候，
第一次和爸爸去看棒球比賽。
他每個週末都和朋友一起打籃球。
我媽媽每天早上去游泳。
冬天時我常和朋友去溜冰。
那位小說家經常跑馬拉松。

I went to see a baseball game with my father for the
first time when I was in elementary school.
He plays basketball with his friends every weekend.
My mother goes swimming every morning.
I often went skating with my friends in winter.
The novelist often runs marathons.

做暖身運動
warm up,
do warm-up
exercise(s)

做有氧運動
do
aerobic exercise(s)

做重量訓練
do
weight training

做瑜伽 / 皮拉提斯
do[practice]
yoga/Pilates

去健身房
go to the gym

接受私人教練訓練
train with
a personal trainer

在跑步機上跑步
run on a treadmill

做深蹲
do squats

做棒式運動
do planks

舉啞鈴 / 舉重
lift a dumbbell/
weights

做仰臥起坐
do sit-ups

做強力步行
power walk

SENTENCES TO USE

在運動前先做暖身運動比較安全。

為了減重，你必須控制飲食和
做有氧運動。

現今很多女性都做皮拉提斯。

她去健身房接受私人教練的訓練。

我每天在家裡做棒式和深蹲。

It is safe to warm up before exercising.

To lose weight, you need to control your diet and do aerobic exercises.

Many women do Pilates these days.

She goes to the gym and trains with a personal trainer.

I do planks and squats at home every day.

登山、露營

去登山
**go hiking,
go mountain climbing**

去攀岩
go rock climbing

購買登山用品
buy hiking supplies

加入登山社
join a climbing club

穿登山鞋 / 登山服 / 戴登山帽
**wear hiking boots/
hiking clothes/an alpine hat**

綁緊登山鞋帶
**tie one's hiking boot
shoelaces tightly**

在夜間登山
go hiking at night

背背包
carry a backpack

SENTENCES TO USE

很多人週末時去登山健行。

她三十幾歲時常去攀岩。

為了開始爬山,他先去購買
登山用品、登山服和登山鞋。

我曾經去夜間登山一次。

Many people go hiking on weekends.

She often went rock climbing in her thirties.

In order to start mountain climbing, he first bought
hiking supplies, hiking clothes, and hiking boots.

I've gone hiking at night once.

大聲吶喊
shout hooray[hurray]

沿著登山步道走
follow
a hiking trail

在山上迷路
get lost
in the mountains

遇難
meet with a disaster

下山
go down
[climb down, descend]
a mountain

* **hiking** 和 **mountain climbing**

　hiking 是指沒有特殊裝備下，沿著山路前行的登山
活動，mountain climbing 是指攜帶齊全裝備後
的登山攻頂活動（包含攀岩）。

SENTENCES TO USE

他們爬到山頂後高聲吶喊著「萬歲」。 They climbed to the top of the mountain and shouted "hooray".

如果你在山上迷路，應該怎麼做？ What should you do if you get lost in the mountains?

那位登山家在從聖母峰下山時遭遇山難。 The climber met with a disaster while climbing down Mount Everest.

因為快日落了，我們就下山了。 We went down the mountain because the sun was about to set.

去露營
go camping

租／買露營車
rent/buy a camper van
[camping car]

把廂型車改裝成露營車
remodel a van
into a camper van
[camping car]

搭／拆帳篷
pitch[set up]/
take down a tent

進入帳篷內
enter[go into] the tent

從帳篷出來
come[step] out of the tent

搭遮陽蓬
put up
an awning

生營火
make
a bonfire

烤肉來吃
have a barbecue,
enjoy a barbecue

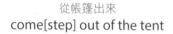

睡睡袋
sleep in
a[one's]
sleeping bag

打開／捲起睡袋
unroll/roll up
one's[the]
sleeping bag

搭／收蚊帳
put up[set up]/
take down
a mosquito net

去車宿露營
go car camping

SENTENCES TO USE

近來越來越多人去露營。
More and more people go camping these days.

他們把廂型車改裝成露營車，
開著它去露營。
They remodeled the van into a camper van and go camping in it.

我們抵達露營區後，先搭了帳篷。
We arrived at the camping site and pitched a tent first.

我們去露營時，通常會烤肉來吃。
When we go camping, we usually have a barbecue.

我們在帳篷裡搭一個蚊帳，
並睡在睡袋裡。
We put up a mosquito net in the tent and slept in a sleeping bag.

在飯店度假
be on a staycation at a hotel

去飯店度假
go on a staycation at a hotel

辦理飯店入住
check in at a hotel

辦理飯店退房
check out of a hotel

在飯店酒吧飲用雞尾酒
drink a cocktail at a hotel bar

要求（～的）客房服務
order room service (for ~)

使用飯店健身中心
use the fitness center in a hotel

在飯店游泳池游泳
swim in the hotel pool

SENTENCES TO USE

上個週末我們去飯店度假兩天一夜。   Last weekend, we were on a staycation at a hotel for 2 days and 1 night.

越來越多人會去飯店度假。   More and more people go on a staycation at hotels.

我們訂了晚餐的客房服務。   We ordered room service for dinner.

我們在飯店的游泳池游泳，並享受水療。   We swam in the hotel pool and enjoyed the spa.

享受水療
enjoy the spa

享受乾式 / 濕式三溫暖
enjoy the dry/wet sauna

欣賞都市夜景
enjoy the night view
of the city

欣賞海景
enjoy
the ocean view

被按摩
get a massage

在浴缸泡半身浴
take a lower-body bath
in the bathtub

吃自助式早餐
have a buffet breakfast

SENTENCES TO USE

這是位於市中心的飯店，
我們可以欣賞都市的夜景。

我在飯店接受足部按摩的服務。

我們泡完半身浴後就上床睡覺了。

他們吃了自助式早餐後就辦理退房了。

It was a hotel in the city center, so we could enjoy the night view of the city.

I got a foot massage at the hotel.

We took lower-body baths and went to bed.

They had a buffet breakfast and then checked out.

去海泳
go swimming
in the sea[ocean]

借海灘傘、陽傘
borrow a beach umbrella,
borrow a parasol

海泳
swim in the sea

在沙灘上玩耍
play on
the sandy beach

躺在沙灘上
lie on
the sandy beach

做沙浴
take a sand bath

曬日光浴
get a tan

衝浪
surf

水肺潛水
scuba dive

淋浴洗去海水鹽份
take a shower
to wash off the salt

SENTENCES TO USE

小時候，每年暑假我都會和父母去海邊游泳。

當我們去海邊時，會先去借一支海灘傘。

即使去海邊，我也不會去海裡游泳，
而是會在沙灘上玩耍。

沙灘上，人們正在做日光浴或沙浴。

很多人在東海（日本海）衝浪。

When I was young, I went swimming in the sea with my parents every summer vacation.

When we go to the beach, we borrow a beach umbrella first.

Even if I went to the beach, I didn't swim in the sea but instead I played on the sandy beach.

On the sandy beach, people were getting a tan or taking a sand bath.

There are a lot of people surfing in the East Sea.

預訂電影票
book a movie ticket,
buy a movie ticket in advance

預訂戲劇 / 音樂劇門票
book a ticket for a play/musical

線上預訂電影票
book[reserve] a movie ticket online

去看電影 / 戲劇 / 音樂劇
go to see a movie/play/musical

看電影 / 戲劇 / 音樂劇
watch a movie/play/musical

一部電影上映 / 上映一部電影
a movie is released/release a movie

在電影院看電影
watch a movie in the theater

看早場、午後場電影
watch a matinee (movie)

看午夜場電影
watch a late-night movie

SENTENCES TO USE

我最大的興趣是看音樂劇。	My biggest hobby is watching musicals.
我等待的電影上映了，於是我在網路上訂了票。	The movie I was waiting for was released, and I booked tickets online.
她喜歡在電影院看電影，而不是在電視上看。	She likes to watch movies at the theater, not on TV.
看早場電影可享折扣。	You can get a discount if you watch a matinee.

在 IPTV/Netflix 上看電影
watch a movie on
IPTV/Netflix

在露天汽車電影院看電影
watch a movie at
a drive-in theater

受邀參加電影首映會
be invited to a movie premiere

參加電影首映會
attend a movie premiere

參加電影節
go to a film festival

SENTENCES TO USE

現在我們不只可以在電影院看電影，
也可以在 IPTV 或 Netflix 上面看。

你在露天汽車電影院看過電影嗎？

我受邀參加那位導演新片的首映會。

她每年秋天都去釜山國際電影節。

Nowadays, we can watch movies not only in theaters but also on IPTV or Netflix.

Have you ever watched a movie at a drive-in theater?

I was invited to the premiere of the director's new film.

She goes to the Busan International Film Festival every fall.

進入劇院
enter
a theater

在入口處驗票
have[get] one's ticket
checked at the entrance

入座
take a seat

將手機調成震動 / 靜音模式
put one's mobile phone on
vibrate/silent mode

在電影開始前觀看廣告
watch commercials
before the movie starts

看完片尾名單
watch all the way to
the end of the credits

關閉手機
turn off one's
mobile phone

邊看電影邊吃爆米花 / 喝飲料
eat popcorn/have a soft drink
while watching a movie

為～熱烈鼓掌
give ~
a big hand

請求謝幕
call the actors and actresses
before the curtain,
clap for a curtain call
（鼓掌要求演員謝幕）

拍手
clap, applaud

為～起立鼓掌
give ~ a standing
ovation

SENTENCES TO USE

進入劇院後，必須將手機調成
靜音模式或關機。

When you enter the theater, you must put
your mobile phone on silent mode or turn it off.

吃爆米花的聲音有時會干擾電影觀賞。

The sound of eating popcorn sometimes interferes
with watching movies.

我會一直看到電影的片尾名單結束。

I watch all the way to the end of the credits.

觀眾為演員們起立鼓掌。

The audience gave the actors a standing ovation.

演出結束後，觀眾鼓掌要求演員謝幕。

After the play was over, the audience clapped for a
curtain call.

7 音樂、演唱會

 069

聽音樂
listen to music

串流播放歌曲
stream
a song

下載歌曲
download
a song

預訂演唱會、演奏會
門票
book[reserve]
a concert ticket

去聽演唱會、演奏會
go to a concert

歡呼
cheer, shout with joy

為～起立鼓掌
give ~ a standing ovation

跟著～一起唱
sing along
(with ~)

要求安可
call for
an encore

演奏樂器 / 鋼琴 / 吉他
play a musical
instrument/the piano/
the guitar

學習演奏樂器 / 鋼琴 / 吉他
learn to play a musical
instrument/the piano/
the guitar

SENTENCES TO USE

我下載了這首歌的 MP3 檔案，常放來聽。 I downloaded the MP3 file of the song and listen to it often.

我以前常去聽演唱會，但最近沒辦法去。 I used to go to concerts often, but these days I can't.

觀眾一邊拍手一邊和音樂家一起歌唱。 The audience is clapping and singing along with the musician.

我從以前就一直想學打鼓。 I've always wanted to learn to play drums.

8 美術、展覽、攝影

畫（～的）畫
draw[paint]
a picture (of ~)

畫風景畫 / 靜物畫
paint
a landscape/a still life

畫～的肖像畫
draw[paint]
a portrait of ~

畫（～的）諷刺畫、似顏繪
draw a caricature (of ~)

畫水彩畫
paint with[in] watercolors, paint a watercolor painting

畫油畫
paint in oils, paint an oil painting

在著色本上著色
color in a coloring book

去看美術展
go to an art exhibition

欣賞展覽品 / 作品 / 畫作 /
雕刻作品
enjoy[appreciate]
exhibits/works/
paintings/sculptures

邊聽講解員說明，邊欣賞作品
appreciate[enjoy] works
listening to a docent's
explanation

購買目錄手冊 / 紀念品
buy a catalogue/a souvenir

預訂展覽門票
book[reserve] an exhibition ticket

SENTENCES TO USE

她從小就喜歡畫畫。
She has been fond of drawing pictures since she was a child.

他有時會到戶外畫風景畫。
He sometimes goes outdoors and paints landscapes.

我為我喜歡的小說家畫
一幅肖像作為禮物送給他。
I drew a portrait of my favorite novelist
and presented it to him.

最近我在練習畫諷刺畫。
I'm practicing drawing caricatures these days.

那位音樂家經常去美術展
欣賞藝術作品。
The musician often goes to art exhibitions and
appreciates the works of art.

拍黑白照
take a black-and-white photo[picture]

用膠卷相機拍照
take a photo[picture] with a film camera

購買專業相機
buy a professional camera

拍照
take a photo,
take a picture

戶外拍攝
go out to take
photos[pictures]

對焦
get into
focus

調整快門速度
adjust the
shutter speed

拍照構圖
compose
a photo

把相機放在三腳架上
put a camera
on a tripod

拍攝模特兒 / 產品
shoot a model/
a product

自拍
take a selfie

使用自拍棒自拍
take a selfie
using
a selfie stick

修飾照片
retouch
[photoshop]
a photo

編輯照片
edit a photo

沖印照片
print a photo

SENTENCES TO USE

我喜歡拍我家貓咪的照片。

她今天去有美麗楓葉的山谷拍照。

你必須學習如何構成一張照片構圖。

我不喜歡自拍。

她在 IG 上發布的照片經過大量修飾。

I enjoy taking pictures of my cat.

She went out to take pictures of a valley with beautiful autumn leaves today.

You need to learn how to compose a photo.

I don't like taking selfies.

The photos she posts on Instagram are heavily retouched.

認養寵物 / 狗（小狗） / 貓
adopt a pet/dog[puppy]/cat

認養被遺棄的狗 / 貓
adopt an abandoned dog/cat

養寵物 / 狗（小狗） / 貓
have[raise] a pet/
dog[puppy]/cat

餵狗 / 貓
feed one's dog/cat

為寵物製作零食
make treats
for one's pet

給寵物零食
give one's
pet treats

和寵物玩
play with
one's pet

購買寵物用品
buy pet
supplies

帶寵物去動物醫院
take one's pet to
an animal hospital

讓寵物打預防針
get one's pet
vaccinated

辦理寵物登記
register
one's pet

為寵物植入晶片
microchip
one's pet

遛狗
walk one's
dog

替狗繫上牽繩
put one's dog
on a leash

SENTENCES TO USE

她認養了一隻被遺棄的狗。
你應該在固定時間餵你的狗和貓。
她親自製作零食給她的狗。
我今天帶我的貓去動物醫院。
當你遛狗的時候，一定要替
牠繫上牽繩，並清理牠的糞便。

She adopted an abandoned dog.
You should feed your dogs and cats at a fixed time.
She makes treats for her dog herself.
I took my cat to the animal hospital today.
When you walk your dog, you must put it on a leash
and clean up after it.

幫狗進行社會化
訓練
socialize
one's dog

幫狗／貓刷牙
brush one's
dog's/cat's teeth

給狗戴嘴套
muzzle
one's dog

（狗）戴嘴套
wear
a muzzle

訓練幼犬定點
大小便
housebreak
a puppy

清理狗大便
clean up after
one's dog

幫狗／貓洗澡
give one's
dog/cat a bath

幫狗／貓修剪毛
get a haircut for
one's dog/cat

組裝／建造貓跳台
assemble/build
a cat tree
[cat tower]

購買／製作貓屋
buy/make
a cat house

清掃貓砂
clean
the cat litter

更換貓砂
change the cat litter

清理貓砂盆
clean the
cat litter box

舉辦寵物葬禮
hold a funeral
for one's pet

讓寵物安樂死
have one's pet
put down

SENTENCES TO USE

在遛猛犬時必須給牠穿戴嘴套。
訓練幼犬定點大小便不是一件容易的事。
我買了一個 DIY 貓跳台並自己組裝。
你必須每天清理貓砂。
我應該多久更換貓砂一次？

Aggressive dogs should wear a muzzle when on a walk.
It is not easy to housebreak a puppy.
I bought a DIY cat tree and built it myself.
You must clean the cat litter every day.
How often should I change the cat litter?

CHAPTER

6

智慧型手機、網路、社群媒體

SMARTPHONE,
THE INTERNET,
SNS

電話、智慧型手機

072

打電話
make a (phone) call

接聽電話
answer[get] a (phone) call,
answer the phone

講電話
talk on
the phone

打視訊電話
make[do]
a video call

傳簡訊
text, send a
text message

傳照片／影片
send a photo
[picture]/video

用 Messenger 聊天
talk on
a messenger app

鎖住智慧型手機
lock one's
smartphone

解鎖智慧型手機
unlock one's
smartphone

滑動解鎖智慧型手機
slide to unlock one's smartphone,
unlock one's smartphone by
sliding to the right

SENTENCES TO USE

我在洗碗，沒有辦法接電話。
I couldn't answer the phone because I was washing the dishes.

位於地球兩端的人們可以藉由撥打視訊電話，面對面地交談。
People on opposite sides of the world can make video calls and talk face to face.

開車時傳簡訊很危險。
It's dangerous to text while driving.

有人說在 Messenger 應用程式交談比打電話更自在。
Some people say that talking on messenger apps is more comfortable than talking on the phone.

他的智慧型手機沒有上鎖。
His smartphone was not locked.

輸入密碼 / 圖形解鎖智慧型手機
enter a password/pattern to unlock one's
smartphone, unlock one's smartphone
by entering a password/pattern

以指紋辨識解鎖智慧型手機
unlock one's smartphone
with a fingerprint

用智慧型手機連接網路
access the Internet with one's
smartphone, use one's smartphone
to access the Internet[to get online]

用智慧型手機上網
use the Internet with one's
smartphone

使用應用程式
use an
application[app]

搜尋應用程式
search for an
application[app]

下載應用程式
download
an application
[app]

安裝應用程式
install
an application
[app]

升級應用程式
update
an application
[app]

刪除應用程式
delete
an application
[app]

SENTENCES TO USE

我用輸入圖形的方式解鎖我的智慧型手機。
現今大部分的人都是透過智慧型手機連接網路。

我正在使用一個可追蹤運動的應用程式。
她下載並安裝了當地圖書館的應用程式。
我刪除了幾個沒有使用的應用程式。

I unlock my smartphone by entering a pattern.
Nowadays, most people access the Internet
with their smartphones.
I'm using an app that tracks my workouts.
She downloaded and installed the local library app.
I deleted several apps that I didn't use.

使用行動銀行
use mobile banking

將智慧型手機投放到電視（用電視看手機畫面）
mirror[cast] one's smartphone screen to a TV

更換智慧型手機的桌面
change the wallpaper of a smartphone

更改智慧型手機的設定
change the settings on one's smartphone

將智慧型手機調成震動 / 靜音模式
put one's smartphone on vibrate/silent mode

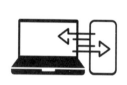

幫手機充電
charge one's phone

幫手機快速充電
fast charge one's phone

將智慧型手機同步至電腦
synchronize one's smartphone with a PC

尋找 Wi-Fi
search for a Wi-Fi network

SENTENCES TO USE

若使用行動銀行，你可以隨時隨地轉帳。
If you use mobile banking, you can transfer money anytime, anywhere.

將智慧型手機投放到電視，就可以用電視看 YouTube。
You can watch YouTube on TV by mirroring your smartphone screen to a TV.

她每天更換智慧型手機的桌面。
She changes her smartphone wallpaper every day.

我們搜尋到一個免費 Wi-Fi，並連接上去。
We searched for a Wi-Fi network and connected to a free one.

電池快沒電了，我必須幫我的手機充電。
The battery is almost dead, so I have to charge my phone.

2 網路、電子郵件

 073

安裝網路
set up a modem,
set up a network

連接網路
connect to the
Internet

使用無線網路
use wireless
Internet

網路中斷連線
the network
is down

連上網站
access a website

上網
surf[browse] the
Internet

在入口網站搜尋資訊
search[look] for information on
a portal site

用 Google 搜尋
google（動詞）

在網站註冊
sign up for a
website

刪除網站帳號
delete one's account from a website,
close one's account at a website

SENTENCES TO USE

現今大部分的人都使用無線網路。　Nowadays, most people use wireless Internet.

當我使用網路時，有時候網路連線會中斷。　Sometimes when I use the Internet, the network is down.

她只要一有空就上網。　She surfs the Internet whenever she has time.

現今人們經常在入口網站搜尋資訊或新聞。　Nowadays, people usually search for information or news on portal sites.

當我想知道什麼事時，馬上用 Google 查詢。　When I want to know something, I google it right away.

登入網站
log in[on] to
a website

登出網站
log out of
a website

輸入用戶 ID 和密碼
enter one's user ID
and password

將網頁加入書籤、我的最愛
bookmark a website,
put a website on one's
favorites list

網路購物
shop online

使用網路銀行
use Internet
banking

玩線上遊戲
play an
Internet[online] game

駭入網站
hack into a website

共用、分享檔案
share a file

複製
copy

貼上
paste

SENTENCES TO USE

我忘記密碼了，
因此我無法登入那個網站。

I couldn't log in to the website because
I forgot my password.

我把那個網站加入書籤了。

I've bookmarked that website.

現今人們大部分的東西
都在網路上購買，包括蔬菜。

Nowadays, people shop online for most things,
including vegetables.

他在休假的時候都玩線上遊戲到天亮。

He plays Internet games until dawn when he's on vacation.

一個國中生駭入那家報社的網站。

A middle school student hacked into the newspaper's website.

建立電子郵件帳戶
create an email account

建立公司的電子郵件帳戶
get an email account from one's
company

登入電子郵件帳戶
log in[on] to one's email account

登出電子郵件帳戶
log out of one's email account

寫電子郵件
write an email

寄電子郵件
send an email

寄電子郵件給自己
send an email to oneself

在電子郵件
附加檔案
attach a file to
an email

回覆電子郵件
reply to an email

轉寄電子郵件
forward
an email

寄副本給～
CC(carbon copy) an email to
someone, CC someone on an
email, copy someone on an email

寄密件副本給～
BCC(blind carbon copy)
an email to someone,
BCC someone on an email

SENTENCES TO USE

我每天會登入那個電子郵件帳戶一次。 I log in to that email account once a day.

現在除了工作以外，我不常寫電子郵件。 These days, I don't usually write emails except for work.

她在電子郵件裡附加了那份檔案。 She attached the file to the email.

今天我回覆了幾封之前的電子郵件。 Today I replied to a few overdue emails.

他寄了副本給他的經理。 He CC'd his manager on the email.

暫存電子郵件
save an email
temporarily

預覽電子郵件
preview
an email

刪除電子郵件
delete an email

永久刪除垃圾郵件
permanently delete
a spam[junk] email

儲存副本
save a copy of
an email

標記為垃圾郵件
mark an email
as spam

清空垃圾桶
empty the trash can

設定電子郵件偏好
set up email preferences

刪除電子郵件帳戶
delete an email account

將電子郵件帳戶改為休眠帳戶
one's email account becomes dormant[inactive]

SENTENCES TO USE

在寄出電子郵件以前，我會先預覽。　I preview an email before I send it.
你應該刪除不必要的電子郵件。　You should delete unnecessary emails.
我把廣告信標記為垃圾郵件。　I mark email ads as spam.
要經常清空電子信箱裡的垃圾。　Empty the trash can in your email box often.
我刪除了我不使用的電子郵件帳戶。　I deleted the email account I wasn't using.

經營部落格
have[run] a blog

在部落格發布文章
write[put] a post on one's blog

加入推特 / Instagram / 臉書
join Twitter/Instagram/Facebook

建立推特 / Instagram / 臉書帳號
create a Twitter/an Instagram/a Facebook account

擁有推特 / Instagram / 臉書帳號
have a Twitter/an Instagram/a Facebook account

使用推特 / Instagram / 臉書
use Twitter/Instagram/Facebook

在推特上推文
tweet

在推特 / Instagram / 臉書上發布～
post ~ on Twitter/Instagram/Facebook

在推特 / Instagram / 臉書上追蹤～
follow ~ on Twitter/Instagram/Facebook

發送 / 接收 DM（私訊）
send/receive a DM(direct message)

在～發布仇恨言論
post hateful comments on ~

SENTENCES TO USE

她經營一個烹飪部落格。
She runs a cooking blog.

我最近加入了 Instagram。
I recently joined Instagram.

我建立了一個臉書帳號，但很快我就刪掉了。
I created a Facebook account but I quickly deleted it.

我不推文，只看其他人發的推文。
I don't tweet; instead I just look at other people's tweets.

在別人的社群媒體留下
仇恨言論的人比我想像得還多。
More people post hateful comments
on other people's SNS than I thought.

開設 YouTube 頻道
open a YouTube channel

拍攝 / 製作影片上傳到 YouTube
shoot/make a video to upload to[on] YouTube

編輯要上傳到 YouTube 的影片
edit a video to upload to[on] YouTube

上傳影片到 YouTube
upload a video to[on] YouTube

在 YouTube 直播
live stream on YouTube

公開打廣告
openly advertise

偷偷打廣告
secretly advertise

點閱數突破～次
have more than ~ views

獲得白銀 / 燦金播放按鈕獎
get[receive] a Silver/Gold Play Button

開箱白銀 / 燦金播放按鈕獎
unbox a Silver/Gold Play Button

將 YouTube 留言置頂
pin a YouTube comment to the top, put a YouTube comment at the top

訂閱人數10萬人 / 100萬人
have a hundred thousand/ one million subscribers

SENTENCES TO USE

那位旅遊作家開設了 YouTube 頻道。 The travel writer opened a YouTube channel.

她每天上傳影片到她的 YouTube 頻道。 She uploads videos to her YouTube channel every day.

那位歌手每週會在 YouTube 直播一次。 The singer live streams on YouTube once a week.

某個人幫貓洗澡的 YouTube 影片擁有超過400萬次的觀看次數。
The YouTube video of someone giving a cat a bath has more than 4 million views.

那個 YouTube 頻道的訂閱人數超過10萬人，獲得了白銀播放按鈕獎。
The YouTube channel received a Silver Play Button with over 100,000 subscribers.

訂閱 YouTube 頻道
subscribe to
a YouTube channel

觀看 YouTube 影片
watch a YouTube video, watch a video on YouTube
以1.25 / 1.5倍速觀看 YouTube 影片
watch a YouTube video at 1.25x/1.5x speed

觀看 YouTube 直播
watch a YouTube
live stream

略過 YouTube 廣告
skip ads
on YouTube

對 YouTube 按「讚」
like a video on
YouTube

針對 YouTube 影片發表
留言
write a comment on
a YouTube video

下載 YouTube 音樂
/ 影片
download music/
videos from
YouTube

擷取 YouTube
影片音軌
extract audio from
a YouTube video

和～分享 YouTube
影片
share
a YouTube
video with ~

在 YouTube / 推特
/ Instagram / 臉書封鎖～
block someone on
YouTube/Twitter/
Instagram/Facebook

SENTENCES TO USE

我訂閱了30多個 YouTube 頻道。

他說話很慢，
所以我用1.25倍速觀看他的 YouTube 影片。

他經常在 YouTube 上看直播。

我看那位 YouTuber 的影片時，不會略過廣告。

我看 YouTube 影片時，都會按下「喜歡」。

有時候我會分享有趣的 YouTube 影片給我的朋友。

I subscribe to over 30 YouTube channels.

He talks slowly,
so I watch his YouTube videos at 1.25x speed.

He often watches YouTube live streams.

I don't skip ads when I watch that YouTuber's videos.

When I watch a YouTube video, I always "like" it.

I sometimes share interesting YouTube videos with
my friends.

CHAPTER

7

大眾交通與駕駛

PUBLIC TRANSPORTATION & DRIVING

公車、地鐵、計程車、火車

搭乘公車 / 地鐵 / 計程車 / 火車 /
快速巴士
take a bus/a subway/a taxi/
a train/an express bus

搭乘公車 / 地鐵 / 計程車
/ 火車 / 快速巴士去～
go to ~ by bus/
subway/taxi/train/
express bus

上公車 / 地鐵
get on a bus/
the subway

下公車 / 地鐵
get off a bus/
the subway

搭計程車、上計程車
get in a taxi
下計程車
get out of a taxi

（趕）搭公車 / 火車
catch a bus/train

錯過公車 / 火車
miss a bus/train

交通卡加值
charge one's
transportation card

購買單程交通卡
buy a single journey ticket

退還單程票保證金
get a refund on the[one's]
single journey ticket
deposit

搭乘雙層巴士
take a
double-decker (bus)

SENTENCES TO USE

她搭計程車去看醫生。
She took a taxi to go see a doctor.

在我上公車時，電話鈴聲響了。
The phone rang as I got on the bus.

當我下計程車時，開始滴雨。
As I got out of the taxi, raindrops began to fall.

我因為錯過8點的火車而上班遲到。
I was late for work because I missed the 8 o'clock train.

今天在上班的路上我必須加值交通卡。
I have to charge my transportation card on my way to
work today.

當你下車時，請去退單程票保證金。
Get a refund on your single journey ticket deposit
when you get off.

查看公車 / 地鐵時間表
check the bus/subway timetable[schedule]

查看公車 / 地鐵路線圖
check the bus/subway (route) map

確認要下車的公車站 / 地鐵站
check the bus stop/subway station to get off

通過地鐵閘門
go through the subway turnstile

從 A 轉乘到 B
transfer from A to B

在公車 / 地鐵找座位
get a seat on the bus/subway

讓座給～
give up one's seat for ~, offer one's seat to ~

坐在博愛座
sit in the priority seat

坐在孕婦專用座
sit in the seat for pregnant women

按下公車上的下車按鈕
press the STOP button on the bus

遺忘某物在地鐵 / 公車 / 計程車上
leave something on the subway/on the bus/in a taxi

坐過站
pass a stop to get off

SENTENCES TO USE

最好事先查看地鐵時刻表。 It's better to check the subway schedule in advance.

我們查看了公車路線圖，
決定在哪裡下車。 We checked the bus route map and decided where to get off.

我搭公車轉地鐵到這裡。 I transferred from the bus to the subway to get here.

那位男孩讓座給一位年長的婦人。 The boy gave up his seat for an elderly woman.

按一下下車按鈕，我們要在這一站下車。 Press the STOP button. We have to get off at this stop.

打電話叫計程車
call a taxi

Uber 叫車
call an Uber

使用應用程式叫計程車
call a taxi using
an app

攔計程車
get[catch, hail]
a taxi

告訴司機目的地
tell one's destination
to the driver,
tell the driver where to
go

（用信用卡／現金）付計程車資
pay the taxi fare[one's taxi ride]
(by credit card/in cash)

領取收據
get a receipt

收找零
get the change

計程車開始跳表計費
start[turn on] the meter

計程車結束跳表計費
turn off the meter

付計程車夜間加成運費
pay taxi fare midnight
surcharge

（計程車司機）拒絕載客
refuse to take
a passenger

SENTENCES TO USE

現今你可以用應用程式叫計程車。
These days, you can call a taxi using an app.

在這條街上很難攔到計程車。
It's hard to catch a taxi on this street.

我非常疲累，以致我在告訴
計程車司機目的地之後就閉上了眼睛。
I was so tired that I closed my eyes after telling
the taxi driver where to go.

我用信用卡付計程車費。
I paid the taxi fare by credit card.

有時候我看到計程車司機拒絕載客。
Sometimes I see taxi drivers who refuse to take
passengers.

購買／預訂火車票／快速巴士車票
buy/book[reserve] a train ticket/
an express bus ticket

選擇火車／快速巴士座位
choose one's seat
on the train/express bus

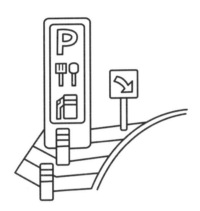

短暫停留在高速公路休息站
stop by[at]
a highway[expressway]
rest[service] area

騎腳踏車／摩托車／電動滑板車
ride a bicycle[bike]/
a motorcycle[motorbike]/
an electric scooter

SENTENCES TO USE

我向來用手機預訂火車票。 | I always book my train tickets by mobile.

在我訂票時，我會選擇快速巴士的座位。 | I chose my seat on the express bus when I booked the ticket.

出差時，他去了高速公路休息站吃午餐。 | During the business trip, he stopped at the highway rest area and ate lunch.

現今很多人騎共享電動滑板車。 | These days, many people ride the electric scooters from scooter-sharing programs.

搭飛機 / 船
take a plane/ship,
get on the plane/ship

搭飛機 / 船去～
go to ~ by plane/ship

預訂機票
book[reserve] a[one's] flight
[plane ticket, airline ticket]

在機場辦理登機手續
check in at the
airport

託運行李
check one's
baggage

通過金屬探測器
go through
the metal detector

辦理出境手續
go through the departure
procedure[process]

登機
board a
flight[plane]

通過旅客登機空橋
go along the passenger boarding
bridge[jet bridge, air bridge]

上 / 下登機梯
go up/down
the ramp

SENTENCES TO USE

我曾經搭船去濟州島旅行。
I have traveled to Jeju Island by ship.

我訂了今年秋天飛往紐約的機票。
I booked a flight to New York this fall.

你最好在飛機起飛前兩小時在機場辦理登機手續。
You should check in at the airport two hours before the flight is scheduled to leave.

她有心律調節器，所以無法通過金屬探測器。
She has a pacemaker, so she can't go through the metal detector.

我在機場辦理出境手續時看到一位名人。
I saw a celebrity while going through the departure procedure at the airport.

把行李放在座位上方置物櫃
put one's baggage[luggage] in the overhead compartment

把行李從座位上方置物櫃拿出來
take one's baggage[luggage] out of the overhead compartment

找到座位坐下
find one's seat
and be seated

取得空服員提供的飲料
get served a
beverage[drink]

吃飛機餐
eat[have] an in-flight
meal[airline meal]

向空服員求助
ask a flight attendant
for help

轉機
change planes

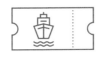

預訂渡輪票
book[reserve]
a ferry

在購票處買渡輪票
buy a ferry ticket at
the ticket office

在驗票口出示
船票和身分證
show one's boarding pass
and ID at the ticket gate

把車子開上汽車渡輪
drive one's car onto
a car ferry

SENTENCES TO USE

上飛機後，我找到座位，
並把行李放進座位上方置物櫃。

After getting on the plane, I found my seat and put my luggage in the overhead compartment.

我喜歡吃飛機餐，因為只有在
旅行時才吃得到。

I like to eat in-flight meals because I only get to eat them when I travel.

在往雷克雅維克的途中，我在倫敦轉機。

I changed planes in London on my way to Reykjavik.

我們訂了渡輪去那個島嶼。

We booked a ferry to the island.

我在驗票口出示船票和身分證後上船。

I showed my boarding pass and ID at the ticket gate and got on the ship.

學習駕駛	上駕駛課	取得駕照	更新駕照	駕駛汽車／貨車／廂型車
learn to drive	take driving lessons	get[obtain] one's driver's license	renew one's driver's license	drive a car/truck/van

繫著安全帶（狀態）
wear one's seat belt

繫上／解開安全帶	直行	倒車	右轉／左轉
fasten/take off one's seat belt	go straight	back one's car, reverse one's car	turn right/left, make a right/left

超車到～前面
cut in front of ~

換車道	迴轉／P 型轉彎	從後視鏡／後照鏡看後方
change lanes	make a U-turn/P-turn	look back in the side mirror/rear-view mirror

SENTENCES TO USE

我在20歲時取得駕照。	I got my driver's license when I was 20.
現在車上每個人都必須繫上安全帶。	Now everyone in the car must wear their seat belt.
當我還是新手駕駛時，換車道並不是一件容易的事。	It was not easy to change lanes when I was a novice driver.
導航説要在前方100公尺處迴轉。	The navigation says to make a U-turn 100 meters ahead.
一輛車在左轉車道超車到其他車輛前面。	A car cut in front of the other cars in the left turn lane.

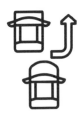
超越
pass ~,
overtake ~

保持安全距離
maintain a safe
distance

遵守速限
keep the speed
limit

加速
speed up,
accelerate

降速
slow down

煞車、踩煞車
brake, put the brakes on,
hit the brakes（急煞）

打方向燈
turn on the turn
signal, put the turn
signal on

開啟危險警示燈
turn on the hazard
lights[four-way flashers]

按喇叭
honk
the[one's]
horn

在指定車道行駛
drive in the designated lane
在外側 / 內側車道行駛
drive in the outside/inside lane

行駛路肩
drive on the shoulder

停靠路肩
stop[pull over] (a car)
on the shoulder

SENTENCES TO USE

你必須保持安全距離並遵守速限，
尤其是在高速公路上。

You have to maintain a safe distance and keep the speed limit, especially on highways.

前車突然停下來，於是我趕緊踩煞車。

The car in front stopped suddenly, so I hit the brakes.

在右轉或左轉前，你必須打方向燈。

You should turn on the turn signals before turning right or left.

你只能在警告其他駕駛有危險時按喇叭。

You should only honk the horn to warn other drivers of danger.

把車子停在路肩是很危險的。

It is dangerous to stop a car on the shoulder.

停車
park, park one's car

接、載～
pick up ~, pick ~ up

載～到某處下車
drop ~ off

安全駕駛
drive safely

遵守 / 違反交通法規
follow[obey]/violate
the traffic laws[rules]

遵守交通號誌
observe the
traffic signal

闖紅燈
run the red light, roll
through the stop sign

超速
speed,
be over the speed limit

被開超速罰單
get a ticket for speeding,
get a speeding ticket

SENTENCES TO USE

她要去接從補習班回來的兒子。

開車的時候一定要遵守交通法規。
那駕駛闖紅燈導致事故發生。
她經常收到超速罰單。

She has to pick up her son coming back from the academy.
When you drive, you must follow the traffic laws.
The driver ran the red light and caused the accident.
She often gets speeding tickets.

疲勞時開車
drive drowsy, drive while tired,
fall asleep at the wheel

疲勞駕駛
drowsy driving, tired driving

在休息站小睡一下
take a nap at a rest area

車子被拖走
have one's car towed

查看行車記錄器
watch[view] the dash cam
[dashboard camera] videos

SENTENCES TO USE

疲勞駕駛是高速公路事故最常見的原因。
Drowsy driving is the most common cause of highway accidents.

我實在太睏了，因此就到休息站小睡一下。
I was so sleepy that I took a nap at the rest area.

他的車子發不動，必須用拖吊車拖走。
His car wouldn't start and he had to have his car towed.

由於我們發生車禍，所以查看行車記錄器的影像。
As we had a car accident, we watched the dash cam video.

酒後開車
drink and drive
酒駕
drunk driving

在酒測臨檢站被抓
get caught at
a sobriety checkpoint

對酒測儀吹氣
breathe[blow] into
a breathalyzer

拒絕酒測
refuse a breathalyzer test

酒駕被捕
be arrested for
drunk driving

吊扣駕照
one's driver's license is suspended

吊銷駕照
have[get] one's driver's license revoked

SENTENCES TO USE

在任何情況下都不應該酒後開車。

You should never drink and drive under any circumstances.

你曾經對酒測儀吹氣過嗎？

Have you ever breathed into a breathalyzer?

他因為酒駕被吊銷駕照。

He got his driver's license revoked for drunk driving.

發生車禍
have a car accident[a traffic accident],
be in a car crash

標示事故位置
mark the location of the accident

發生輕微擦撞事故
have a fender bender

車輛故障
break down

車輛爆胎
have a flat tire, a tire goes flat

聯絡保險公司
contact one's insurance company

SENTENCES TO USE

在看完棒球比賽回家的路上，她發生了輕微擦撞的事故。
She had a fender bender on her way back from the baseball game.

在停車場正準備出發時，我發現車子爆胎了。
I was about to leave the parking lot when I found out that I had a flat tire.

發生交通事故時，你應該聯絡保險公司。
If you are in a car accident, you should contact your insurance company.

加油
put gas
in one's car

自助加油
put gas in one's
car oneself

把車子的油箱加滿
fill up (one's car),
gas up one's car

打開油箱蓋
open the fuel
door

（委託別人）洗車
have[get] one's
car washed

通過自動洗車機
go through an
automatic car wash

手工洗車
handwash one's car,
wash one's car by hand

請人檢查車子
have[get] one's
car checked

請人修理車子
have[get] one's car
repaired[fixed]

報廢車子
scrap
one's car

SENTENCES TO USE

在出發去旅行前，我把車子的油加滿。
你必須打開油箱蓋才能加油。
在把車加滿油之後，有時我會開去
自動洗車。
他親自手洗自己的車子。
她的車子故障了，因此她去汽車修理
廠請人修車。

I filled up my car before I left for the trip.
You have to open the fuel door to put gas in your car.
I sometimes go through an automatic car wash after
putting gas in my car.
He handwashes his car himself.
Her car broke down so she went to the repair shop to
have it repaired.

檢查 / 更換機油 / 煞車油
have[get] the engine oil/brake oil checked/changed

補充雨刷水
add[refill] washer fluid[windshield wiper fluid]

補充 / 更換冷卻劑
add/change coolant, have coolant added/changed

更換空氣濾芯
change one's[the] car air filter, have one's[the] car air filter changed

檢查 / 更換輪胎
have the tires checked/rotated

做車輪定位
get a wheel alignment, get the wheels aligned

更換雨刷
change the wipers[windshield wipers], have the wipers [windshield wipers] changed

檢查冷氣
have the air conditioner checked

貼車窗隔熱紙
have one's[the] car windows tinted

用吸塵器清潔車輛內部
vacuum the interior of one's car

清潔腳踏墊
clean the floor mats

SENTENCES TO USE

你應該每一萬公里就更換一次機油。 You should get the engine oil changed every 10,000 kilometers.

我可以自己補充雨刷水。 I can add washer fluid myself.

她從去年開始更加頻繁地更換汽車的空氣濾芯。 She's been changing her car air filter more often since last year.

每次去換汽車機油時，我都會請人檢查輪胎。 Every time I have my car engine oil changed, I get the tires checked.

他有時會用吸塵器清潔車子內部。 He sometimes vacuums the interior of his car.

CHAPTER

8

社會與政治

SOCIETY & POLITICS

079

_____發生車禍
have a car accident,
be in a car crash

發生輕微擦撞事故
have a fender
bender

被車撞
be hit[be run
over] by a car

列車脫軌
a train derails[is
derailed]

飛機失事
an airplane
crashes

船隻沉沒
a ship sinks

地鐵發生火災
a fire breaks out in[on]
the subway

發生火災
a fire breaks out

建築倒塌
a building collapses

受困在倒塌的建築下
be trapped under
a collapsed building

發生爆炸
an explosion occurs

瓦斯爆炸
a gas explosion

SENTENCES TO USE

今天我在下班回家的路上發生了輕微的擦撞事故。
I had a minor fender bender on my way home from work today.
那位外送員在運送食物時被車撞到。
The delivery man was hit by a car while delivering food.
今天那座城市的列車脫軌，很多人因此受傷。
Many people were injured today when a train derailed in the city.
當飛機失事時，往往導致許多乘客失去性命。
Often, when an airplane crashes, many of the passengers lose their lives.
如果地鐵發生火災，很可能造成大量人員傷亡。
If a fire breaks out on the subway, it can lead to a mass mortality event.

被燒燙傷
get burned,
burn oneself,
get a burn

遭受一度 / 二度 / 三度燒燙傷
get a first-degree/second-
degree/third-degree burn

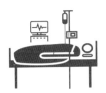

全身被燒燙傷
burn oneself
all over

掉入水中
fall into
the water

溺死
drown

從施工現場 / 公寓陽台 /
建築屋頂等墜落
fall from[off]
a construction site/
an apartment balcony/
a building rooftop …

執勤中受傷 / 死亡
get injured/die
at work[on duty]

遭受工傷
suffer an
industrial injury

過勞死
work oneself
to death

受創傷後壓力症候群(PTSD)
所苦
suffer from PTSD(post-
traumatic stress syndrome)

發生醫療事故
a medical
accident occurs

打電話叫救護車
call
an ambulance

被載去急診室
be taken to the ER
(emergency room)

SENTENCES TO USE

小時候我曾經被熱水燙傷。

那次意外有幾個人溺死在河裡。

在執勤中受傷的人應獲得適當補償。

現今發生醫療事故時，患者必須提出證明。

人們打電話叫救護車，那男子就被載去急診室。

I once got burned by hot water when I was young.

Several people drowned in the river in the accident.

Compensation for people who get injured on duty should be done properly.

Now, when a medical accident occurs, the patient has to prove it.

People called an ambulance, and the man was taken to the ER.

人經歷自然災害
experience[live through]
a natural disaster,
be hit[struck] by a natural disaster

地區遭受自然災害
suffer (from) a natural disaster,
be hit[struck] by a natural disaster

人因暴雨 / 洪水而受害
be affected by heavy rain/flood

地區因暴雨 / 洪水而受害 / 遭受破壞 / 被摧毀
be affected by[suffer from]/be destroyed by/
be devastated by heavy rain/flood

事物因暴雨 / 洪水而受損
be damaged by heavy rain/flood

人因颱風而受害
be hit by[be affected by] a typhoon

地區因颱風而受害 / 遭受破壞 / 被摧毀
be hit by[be affected by]/
be destroyed by/be devastated by
a typhoon

事物因颱風而受損
be damaged by a typhoon

人因酷暑而受害
be caught in
[be affected by]
a heat wave

地區因酷暑而受害
be affected by
[suffer from] a heat
wave

人因寒流而受害
be caught in
[be affected by]
a cold wave

地區因寒流而受害
be affected by
[suffer from]
a cold wave

人因暴雪而受害
be affected by heavy snow

地區因暴雪而受害
be affected by[suffer from]
heavy snow

人因雪崩 / 山崩而受害
be caught in[be affected by] an
avalanche/a landslide

地區因雪崩 / 山崩而受害 / 遭受破壞
be affected by[suffer from]/be
destroyed by an avalanche/a landslide

人因乾旱而受苦
be affected by drought

地區因乾旱而受害
suffer from[be affected by] drought

人因森林大火而受害
be affected by a forest fire

地區或事物因森林大火而受害 / 遭受破壞
be affected by/be destroyed by a forest fire

人因地震 / 海嘯而受害
be affected by an earthquake/a tsunami

地區因地震 / 海嘯而受害 / 遭受破壞 / 被摧毀
be affected by/be destroyed by/be devastated by
an earthquake/a tsunami

事物因地震 / 海嘯而受損
be damaged by an earthquake/a tsunami

人因火山爆發而受害
be affected by a volcanic
eruption

地區因火山爆發而受害 / 遭受破壞
be affected by/be destroyed by
a volcanic eruption

人因黃沙 / 細塵而受害
be affected by yellow dust/fine dust

地區因黃沙 / 細塵而受害
be affected by[suffer from] yellow dust/
fine dust

人因地陷而受害
be affected by a sinkhole

地區因地陷而受害 / 遭受破壞
be affected by/be destroyed
by a sinkhole

SENTENCES TO USE

那個村莊因暴雨而遭受極大破壞。
數百人在那次地震中受害。

The village was badly damaged by this heavy rain.
Hundreds of people were affected by the earthquake.

犯下罪行
commit a crime

逃跑
flee, run away

被逮捕
be[get] arrested

偷
steal ~

搶劫 A 的 B
rob A of B

扒竊
pickpocket

詐騙
commit fraud,
con, swindle

偽造～元紙鈔
counterfeit a ~ bill

非法賭博
do illegal
gambling

向～行賄
bribe ~, give[offer]
a bribe to ~

盜用、貪污
embezzle ~

以語音釣魚的方式詐騙
commit fraud
with voice phishing

SENTENCES TO USE

那男子犯下罪行後逃跑了。 The man committed a crime and ran away.

那家商店櫃檯裡的現金都被搶光了。 The store was robbed of all the cash on the counter.

那位喜劇演員因為非法賭博而被禁止在電視上演出。 The comedian was suspended from appearing on TV for illegal gambling.

軍火商向與國防業務有關的政客們行賄。 The arms dealer bribed politicians involved in defense.

現今仍有許多人以語音釣魚的方式行騙。 There are still many people who commit fraud with voice phishing these days.

進行網路犯罪
commit cyber crime

毀損名譽
harm[damage, defame]
someone's reputation

洩漏業務機密
leak[reveal, give away] company
confidential information

妨礙執行公務
obstruct the execution of official duties, interfere
with a public official in the execution of his/her
duty

誣告
make a false
accusation,
falsely accuse

偽造私人文件
forge a private
document

抄襲
plagiarize ~

酒後開車
drink and drive

無照駕駛
drive without
a license

有「路怒症」
have road rage

肇事逃逸
hit and run

SENTENCES TO USE

那名 YouTuber 因毀損一位女演員的
名譽而被判有罪。

The YouTuber was found guilty of defaming an
actress's reputation.

他因妨礙執行公務罪被罰款。

He was fined for obstructing the execution of official duties.

那名女子被發現誣告另一名男子性侵害。

The woman was found to have falsely accused the other
man of sexual assault.

那位暢銷書作者被懷疑抄襲了一
本不太受歡迎的書。

The author of the best seller was suspected of plagiarizing a
less popular book.

那名男子被警察抓到無照駕駛。

The man was caught driving without a license by the police.

吸毒
take drugs

走私毒品
smuggle drugs

毆打
hit ~, assault ~

犯下性犯罪
commit a sex crime

性騷擾
sexually
harass

強暴猥褻行為、猥褻
indecently assault,
molest

性侵害
sexually assault,
rape

約會暴力
commit dating violence,
physically assault ~ while dating

性交易
pay for sex,
prostitute（賣淫）

偷拍
secretly record
videos

跟蹤騷擾
stalk

SENTENCES TO USE

那男子因涉嫌吸毒和走私毒品而被移交法院審判。
The man was put on trial on charges of taking drugs and smuggling them.
那名政治人物的政治生涯因為犯下性犯罪而告終。
The politician's political life ended because he committed a sex crime.
犯下約會暴力的人大部分是男性，但有時也會有女性。
It's mostly men who commit dating violence, but sometimes women commit it, too.
那名歌手因為偷拍及散布影片而被判入獄服刑。
The singer was sentenced to prison for secretly recording videos and distributing them.
主流觀點認為應強化對跟蹤騷擾行為的處罰。
The prevailing view is that the punishment for stalking should be increased.

綁架、誘拐
kidnap ~

販賣〜（人口）
traffic in ~

虐待兒童 / 老人 / 動物
abuse[mistreat] a child/
an old man/an animal

殺害
murder ~, kill ~

殺人未遂
the attempt to
murder has failed

犯下連續殺人
commit serial
murders

連續殺人犯
a serial killer

棄屍
dump a body

在〜放火、縱火
set ~ on fire,
set fire to ~

犯下恐怖攻擊
commit an act
of terrorism

自殺炸彈恐攻
carry out a suicide
bombing

SENTENCES TO USE

過去有個老師綁架殺害自己學生的事件。

In the past, there was an incident in which a teacher kidnapped and killed his student.

虐待動物的人很可能也會虐待人。

People who abuse animals are likely to abuse people.

那個男子在5年當中殺死10個人。
換言之，他是個連續殺人犯。

The man killed 10 people in five years.
In other words, he was a serial killer.

一個喝醉的人半夜放火燒了那道門。

A drunk man set the gate on fire in the middle of the night.

那名恐怖份子以自殺炸彈進行恐怖攻擊。

The terrorist carried out a suicide bombing.

3 法律、審判

指控、控告
accuse ~, sue ~

起訴
indict ~

對～提起民事訴訟
file a civil suit[lawsuit] against ~

對～提起刑事訴訟
file a criminal suit against ~

守法
observe[abide by] the law

違法
break[violate] the law

對～提起離婚訴訟
file for divorce from ~

審理
try

辯護
plead, defend

作證
give testimony

檢察官求刑～
the prosecutor
demands[asks for] ~

裁決
judge

被判有罪 / 無罪
be found guilty/not guilty

SENTENCES TO USE

你必須盡可能地守法。	You must abide by the law as much as possible.
那位歌手控告網路酸民。	The singer sued Internet trolls.
那名女子對丈夫提起離婚訴訟。	The woman filed for divorce from her husband.
那位檢察官對被告求刑7年徒刑。	The prosecutor demanded a seven-year prison term for the defendant.
在經過5年的審理後， 那名男子最終被判無罪。	The man was eventually found not guilty after a trial that lasted five years.

判決
sentence
被判刑～年 / 無期徒刑 / 死刑
be sentenced to ~ years in prison/life in prison/death
被判緩刑
be sentenced to probation

被判處罰金
be fined,
be sentenced to a fine

入獄、被關進監獄
go to jail/prison, be sent to[be put into] jail/prison

服刑～（期間）
serve ~ in prison

被單獨監禁
be put into solitary confinement

申請保釋
apply for bail
獲交保釋放
be released on bail

被減刑為～
be reduced [commuted] to ~

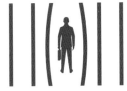

（成為模範囚犯）獲得假釋
be paroled, be released on parole (because he/she is a model prisoner)

獲得赦免
be pardoned

（向上級法院）上訴
appeal
(to a higher court)

SENTENCES TO USE

法院判處疏忽照顧孩童導致女兒死亡的女子入監服刑20年。

他因酒駕被處罰鍰。

他在監獄裡服刑12年，出獄後又犯了另一條罪。

那犯人在服刑10年後因成為。模範囚犯而獲得假釋

她被判有罪，但又立即提出上訴。

The court sentenced the woman to 20 years in prison for child neglect leading to the death of her daughter.

He was fined for drunk driving.

He served 12 years in prison and committed another crime right after he was released.

The prisoner was released on parole after 10 years in prison because he had been a model prisoner.

She was found guilty but appealed immediately.

投票
vote

透過選舉選出～
elect ~

舉行選舉
hold an election

舉行總統選舉
hold a presidential election

舉行國會議員選舉
hold legislative[parliamentary] elections

舉行地方政府選舉
hold local government elections

舉行重選 / 補選
hold re-elections /
by-elections

事前投票
vote in advance of
the election day

提前投票
early voting

棄權投票
abstain from voting

把票投給～（候選人）
vote for ~

劃記選票
fill out[in] a ballot

把選票投入投票箱
put a ballot in
a ballot box

拍下投票認證照
take photos as proof
of voting

SENTENCES TO USE

投票是民主國家人民的權力與義務。
It is the right and duty of the people of a democratic country to vote.

在總統直選制中，人民直接選出總統。
In the direct presidential election system, the people directly elect the president.

在那個國家，總統選舉每5年舉辦一次，
國會議員選舉每4年舉行一次。
In the country, presidential elections are held every five years and legislative elections are held every four years.

上個月，我們市舉辦了市長補選。
Last month, our city held a by-election for mayor.

我已進行了事前投票。
I voted in advance of the election day.

競選總統
run for the presidency, run for president

競選國會議員
run for a seat in the National Assembly

競選市長
run for mayor

登記為候選人
register as a candidate

Election

不競選連任
not seek
re-election

支持候選人
support
a candidate

參加競選活動
campaign for election,
go on a campaign

進行民意調查
conduct
a (public opinion) poll

回應民意調查
respond to
a (public opinion) poll

計票
count votes

宣布選舉結果
announce the result
of the election

勝選 / 敗選
win/lose an
election

領取當選證書
receive a certificate
of election

SENTENCES TO USE

那位演員以前曾經競選過國會議員。

那位國會議員宣布他不會競選連任。

你有支持的候選人嗎？

今天我回應了一份關於即將到來的
總統大選的民意調查。

選舉結束一小時後，選區開始開票。

The actor ran for a seat in the National Assembly before.

The lawmaker announced he was not seeking re-election.

Is there a candidate you are going to support?

Today I responded to a poll about the upcoming
presidential election.

The election district began counting votes an hour
after the election was over.

5 宗教

相信～（宗教）
believe in ~

上教堂／教會／佛寺
go to Catholic church/church/Buddhist temple

改信
convert to ~

天主教

（去教堂）
望彌撒
go to mass

在網路上望彌撒
attend mass online

禱告
pray

誦念玫瑰經
pray the rosary

聽佈道
listen to the
sermon

在胸口畫十字
cross oneself

SENTENCES TO USE

那名女子改信她先生的宗教——新教，
因此他們可以在教會裡結婚。

The woman converted to her husband's religion,
Protestantism, so they could be married in the church.

他每個週日都去望彌撒。

He goes to mass every Sunday.

她吃飯前向來會在自己胸口畫十字。

She always crosses herself before eating meals.

帶面紗
wear a veil

決定洗禮名
decide on a baptismal
name[Christian name]

受洗
be baptized

領聖餐
take communion

懺悔
go to confession,
confess (one's sins)

成為教父 / 教母
become a godfather/
godmother

SENTENCES TO USE

女性信徒在教堂裡帶著面紗祈禱。
我媽媽在60幾歲時受洗成為天主教徒。
如果你是一位天主教徒，
你會向神父懺悔一切嗎？

Female believers pray in the cathedral wearing veils.
My mother was baptized a Catholic in her sixties.
If you were a Catholic, would you confess everything
to a priest?

新教

去教會、上教會
**go to church,
attend church**

參加禮拜
attend a service

06:00 AM

參加清晨禮拜
**attend an early
morning service**

舉行家庭禮拜
**hold[give] family
worship**

參加地區禮拜
**have a district service,
have a service with the same
district group**

參加網路禮拜
attend online worship service

唱讚美詩歌
sing a hymn

聽佈道
**listen to
the sermon**

奉獻
**give an offering,
make an offering of money**

SENTENCES TO USE

國中時我曾經上過幾個月的教會。

I attended church for several months when I was in middle school.

因為 COVID-19的關係，最近我們參加網路禮拜。

Because of COVID-19, we attend online services these days.

在禮拜當中，我最喜歡唱讚美詩歌。

I like singing hymns during the services most of all.

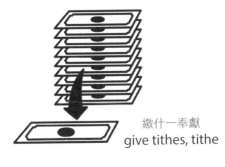

繳什一奉獻
give tithes, tithe

接受教理課程
take a baptism class

成為主日學老師
be a Sunday school
teacher

參加復興聚會
attend a revival
meeting[assembly]

傳福音
evangelize

有靈修時間
have a quiet[Bible] time

閱讀 / 抄寫聖經
read/transcribe
the Bible

研讀聖經、參加聖經讀經班
study the Bible,
participate in a Bible study group

SENTENCES TO USE

他每個月繳什一奉獻。
她做主日學老師好幾年了。
最近我每天抄寫聖經一個小時。

He gives tithes every month.
She has been a Sunday school teacher for several years.
I transcribe the Bible for an hour every day these days.

佛教

參加法會
attend a Buddhist service

供佛祝禱
pray to Buddha, offer a Buddhist prayer, worship in the Buddhist temple

合掌於胸前
put one's hands together in front of the chest [as if in prayer]

數著念珠祈禱
count one's beads

（出聲）讀誦佛經
read the Buddhist scriptures (out loud)

跪拜
make a deep bow

做108拜
make one hundred and eight bows

聽僧侶講佛法
listen to the monk's sermon

捐獻、捐獻金錢／米／
建築／財產
give alms, donate[offer] money/ rice/a building/property …

燒香
burn incense

點亮燭火
light a candle

點亮蓮燈
light a lotus lantern

SENTENCES TO USE

那位女子為了她的子女去供佛祝禱。 The woman prays to Buddha for her children.

那位僧侶閉著眼睛坐著數念珠祈禱。 The monk was counting his beads while sitting with his eyes closed.

佛教徒們正大聲讀誦佛經。 The Buddhists were reading the Buddhist scriptures out loud.

她每天早上做108拜。 She makes one hundred and eight bows every morning.

我睡前會在 YouTube 上聽僧侶講佛法。 I listen to monks' sermons on YouTube before I go to bed.

6 軍隊

084

當兵、入伍
join the military,
enlist (in ~)

加入陸軍 / 海軍 / 空軍 /
海軍陸戰隊
enlist in the army/navy/
air force/marine corps

服兵役
serve in the military,
do one's military service

做身體檢查
get[receive] a physical
examination

接受新兵訓練
do boot camp, receive
basic training at boot camp

被分配到部隊
be assigned to a unit

敬禮
salute,
give a salute

配戴軍牌
wear dog tags

點名
take[make, have]
a roll call

SENTENCES TO USE

入伍後，他們被送到新兵訓練營一個月。

After joining the military, they were sent to boot camp for one month.

那位歌手在5月底入伍。

The singer enlisted at the end of May.

我的父親服38個月的兵役。

My father served in the military for 38 months.

在新兵訓練營接受基本訓練後，
他們被分配到部隊。

They were assigned to units after receiving basic training at boot camp.

行軍
march

跑步
march at double-quick

站崗
mount guard, stand sentry,
stand guard

夜間站崗
keep a night watch

報上姓名、官階 、編號
give one's name, rank,
and serial number

12:00 AM

進行夜間訓練
do[take part in] night training
[nighttime training]

SENTENCES TO USE

在夏日白天行軍真的很辛苦。

兩名士兵在彈藥庫前站崗。

他從半夜12點站崗到凌晨3點。

那個部隊從今年開始進行夜間訓練。

It's really hard to march during the day in summer.

Two soldiers were standing guard in front of the ammunition depot.

He kept a night watch from 12 a.m. to 3 a.m.

The unit began doing night training this year.

進行冬季 / 夏季訓練
do[take part in] winter/summer training

進行游擊訓練
do[take part in] guerrilla training

唱軍歌
sing a military song[war song]

收到慰問信
receive a letter of consolation

面會
visit, come to visit

去休假 / 休假中
go/be on leave

回部隊
return to one's unit

在災區參與救災
take part in relief work in disaster areas

欣賞勞軍表演
enjoy the show at a military camp

被送到國軍醫院
be taken to a military hospital

退伍
be discharged (from the military service)

逃離部隊
go AWOL(absent without leave), desert[run away]
from the army[military]

去禁閉室
be confined[locked up] in the guardhouse

SENTENCES TO USE

我們進行了5天4夜的游擊訓練。

上個週末，我的女友來
我的部隊與我面會。

明天是他結束
休假回部隊的日子。

他預計下個月退伍。

據報導，一名男子在
逃離部隊20年後自首。

We did guerrilla training for four nights and five days.

Last weekend, my girlfriend came to
visit me at my unit.

Tomorrow is the day he returns to
his unit after being on leave.

He is scheduled to be discharged next month.

A man reportedly deserted from
the military and turned himself in after 20 years.

A

C

D

H

M

Q

R

S

T

X

Y

Z

EZ TALK

圖解英語會話關鍵動詞

作　　　者 ： 徐寧助
譯　　　者 ： 謝宜倫
責 任 編 輯 ： 謝有容
裝 幀 設 計 ： 初雨有限公司（ivy_design）
內 頁 排 版 ： 初雨有限公司（ivy_design）
行 銷 企 劃 ： 張爾芸

發 　行 　人 ： 洪祺祥
副 總 經 理 ： 洪偉傑
副 總 編 輯 ： 曹仲堯
法 律 顧 問 ： 建大法律事務所
財 務 顧 問 ： 高威會計師事務所

出　　　版 ： 日月文化出版股份有限公司
製　　　作 ： EZ叢書館
地　　　址 ： 臺北市信義路三段151號8樓
電　　　話 ： (02) 2708-5509
傳　　　真 ： (02) 2708-6157
網　　　址 ： www.heliopolis.com.tw
郵 撥 帳 號 ： 19716071日月文化出版股份有限公司

總 　經 　銷 ： 聯合發行股份有限公司
電　　　話 ： (02) 2917-8022
傳　　　真 ： (02) 2915-7212

印　　　刷 ： 中原造像股份有限公司
初　　　版 ： 2023年3月
定　　　價 ： 380元
I　S　B　N ： 978-626-7238-42-4

圖解英語會話關鍵動詞 / 徐寧助著；謝宜倫
譯 . -- 初版 . -- 臺北市：日月文化出版股份有
限公司 , 2023.03
296 面 ; 23×17 公分 . -- (EZ talk:)
譯自： 거의 모든 행동 표현의 영어
ISBN 978-626-7238-42-4 (平裝)
1.CST: 英語 2.CST: 會話 3.CST: 動詞

805.188　　　　　　　　　　112000059

거의 모든 행동 표현의 영어
Copyright ⓒ2022 by Suh Young Jo
All rights reserved.
Original Korean edition published by Saramin.
Chinese(traditional) Translation rights arranged with Saramin.
Chinese(traditional) Translation Copyright ⓒ2023 by Heliopolis Culture Group Co., Ltd
through M.J. Agency, in Taipei.

◎版權所有，翻印必究
◎本書如有缺頁、破損、裝訂錯誤，請寄回本公司更換